Lawrence Russell. Born in Northern Ireland, educated in the U.K, Canada, and California. Playwright, fiction writer, critic, musician and multi-media artist. Formerly Professor of Writing & Film, University of Victoria. Twice winner of the Canadian Broadcasting Corporation's Literary Competition. His stage plays have been produced in all the major Canadian venues, including the National Arts Theatre (Ottawa) and the Stratford (Ontario) Festival's 3rd Stage. His drama and electronic sound-text compositions have been broadcast on the C.B.C., A.B.C., Radio Canada International, N.P.R. (National Public Radio, US), the Pacifica Radio Network and other broadcast networks. Books include *Penetration* (5 plays), *Repeat This & You're Dead* (stories), *Radio Brazil* (novel) and the recent non-fiction work *Outlaw Academic* (criticism/metafiction/autobiography). LR's website is: culturecourt.com

For my daughter, Thea Celeste

LAWRENCE RUSSELL
Temple of the Two Moons

This novel is entirely a work of fiction.
The names, characters and incidents portrayed in it are the work of the
author's imagination. Any resemblance to actual persons, living or dead,
events or localities is entirely coincidental.

Temple of the Two Moons
Copyright © Lawrence Russell 2023
All rights reserved.

Published By
THE TERMINAL PRESS

First Edition

ISBN: 978-1-990682-03-2

Contents

1: The Sea Dragon

I get a call from Kelly at Control and he says, "Pack your bag, Caine, you're needed in Yokohama."

It wasn't Yokohama actually — it was Kawasaki, the port beside Yoko. That's Tokyo Bay, Japan. An autoliner called the Sea Dragon needed a quartermaster because the one they had fell over-board after they left Korea with a few hundred cars. They were picking up more in Japan. The Sea Dragon was a Horizon class carrier, so could carry quite a few vehicles. Thirteen decks, say 7,000 if fully loaded, although these days with the depressed global market, it probably wouldn't be. Chances were there'd be some used stuff mixed in too. Kelly said there were some luxury cars on the manifest. Luxury? I guessed we'd be stopping off in the Middle East, then. The sheiks liked upscale motors. These would be Japanese or recycled Euro models.

I resisted the temptation to drink on the flight out, read a paperback I'd found abandoned on a seat in the boarding lounge. The story was quite good. Bit literary perhaps because I fell asleep and this made the flight easier and kept my mind clean. Sometimes I have trouble with booze, the sailor's disease. Might as well be honest — I'd been black-listed for the past year due to an incident where I had a fight with the lst officer of the... well, let's not go into that. Like Mike Tyson said, "Everybody's got a plan until they get punched in the face."

He says I punched him but that's not how I remember it. I had the plan and he didn't like it.

So what are my duties as quartermaster? For this gig I'm more like the army sort. I can navigate and do maps but these guys want me to be flexible, do lots of things including supervising the loading and unloading of the vehicles. The Dragon is what we call a 'RoRo', which means a 'roll on, roll off' ship. Cars and trucks can be driven on and off the decks directly, no pissing around with cranes and hoists. We took on about 1,800 new cars and SUVs — mostly Nissans and Mazdas, and a smorgasbord of good condition used, stuff like Lexus and Acura, low kilometers, might as well be new. And there were a few collectibles, vintage orders that people had bought when visiting Japan.

There was one beauty, a 1941 black Lincoln supposedly owned by the Emperor Hirohito's family, a twin of the flashy green model recently auctioned off that the old film noir star Rita Hayworth owned. Two door hardtop, rear fender skirts, continental kit... and unlike Rita's, this Hirohito model still had the original V-12 motor.

I'm getting ahead of myself here, though.

It's a nice day and you could smell the cherry blossoms in the air, despite the pungent industrial odor of the port. I'm standing at the boarding ramp with a member of the crew who's operating the digital photo log, the machine that records the cars for the manifest as they load. Easy, not like the old days. So I'm almost asleep on my feet because I'm jet-lagged and bored shitless. We use a team of local drivers to do the loading, both male and female, but you know, there isn't a decent looking bird among them.

I'm yawning when the Captain appears at my shoulder, surprises the hell out of me.

"Mister Caine," he says. "How nice to see you.'"

"Captain," I say. "Have we met?"

"No, sir. I read your dossier with interest... no need to be alarmed. I like experienced sailors."

This was good to know. Kelly, back in Control, said my resume read like a 'fucking crime novel'. Joking, of course. Otherwise I would've been booted out of the Union. Well, there might be still time for that.

"What happened to Mishima?" I say. "If you don't mind me asking."

"Didn't they say? He went overboard."

"That's tragic."

"Just so, Mr. Caine. Tragic perhaps, incompetent most definitely."

The way he said this left no room for further enquiry.

Ekzetera was a classic. No, he didn't have a wooden leg, although he did have a buggered eye. No patch, just a lizard slit, so the eyeball was white. Maybe it was glass. Nobody I asked seemed to know for sure but then most of these beggars on the crew couldn't even pronounce his name, got to calling him 'X' or the 'Big X'. He wasn't big. Five seven or eight, short by today's normal in the western world. Kelly said he was from one of those small republics on the Black Sea that sometimes exist, sometimes not, so he could be a sort of Russian or Turk... or anything he liked. His English wasn't bad. Better than mine and I'm Canadian.

"What's on Deck 13?" I say. "Korean models?"

"Yes, luxury cars. Generally heavier."

O.k. Heavy stuff on the bottom, keep the ship trim and steady. It did occur to me that Korea isn't generally associated with 'luxury' autos but then, these days, these Asian manufacturers could surprise you with anything.

The dock area was one huge parking lot. There were thousands of cars parked in blocks and truck transporters were bringing them in all the time. It was like watching a board game. Off to the left there was a block of 'collectibles'. Not many this particular day, but some.

X nods that direction, says, "There's a car over there I want you to load."

He's holding up a set of keys. They're turning slowly left, then right, like a wind chime.

"Me?" I say. "Me... you want me to drive it on board?"

"You, quartermaster. It's a special car. I don't trust these clowns."

It was the Hirohito Lincoln. Standard transmission. Kids today only know automatics and most of the loaders were kids.

"Top deck," he says. "Make room if there isn't room, o.k.?"

There was room. Needless to say, I did wonder, eh. But it's not for the rehabilitated to wonder, so I took the keys and went and got the Lincoln. Left-hand drive, so maybe this was why X wanted me to drive it on board as Japan is right hand drive and these kids might have problems with this as well. Truthfully, it was a bit of a struggle for me because I hadn't driven a standard since I had a Volkswagon Beetle and a girlfriend who smoked French cigarettes. Nice interior, though. Leather, very cushy. Nice fragrance too, like it had been driven by a princess or for a princess.

Actually, this was the last vehicle to be loaded. The azi thrusters were already revving and the mooring lines cast off by the time I got Hirohito parked and put the blocks under the wheels. Usually you leave the keys in the ignition so the destination drivers can just hop in, start the car up, drive it to the dispersal lot on the dock but Ekzetera had told me to bring the keys back to him. Naturally I was thinking this car must be his, something he scored at a Tokyo car auction or from an ad in *The Herald* or more likely *The Japan Maritime Daily*. But maybe not. Maybe he was just making sure it didn't get dented, have the real owner and his insurance company get on his back.

It was then that I got the surprise of my life, matey. Someone had been hiding in the back, on the floor, tight to the seats. Never noticed him, even when I turned my head to reverse before leaving the dock. The person pushed the seat forward, opened the passenger door, stepped out. Young, Japanese and androgynous, and my first thought was this is the chauffeur because he was wearing a man's suit and the sort of cap a chauffeur might wear.

But it wasn't a guy at all. The doll face and the cheeky mouth put paid to that.

She scowls at me, says, "Take me to the Big X."

Bloody rights I will, I think. There'll be hell to pay for this. Had to be one of the loading drivers who was taking a kip in the car and now we've got a goddamn stowaway.

"You're in shit," I say. "Next port of call is Singapore."

"Not for me," she says. "Like my car?"

"Beauty... but you're not old enough to drive, are you?"

"Take me to the Captain, *manuke*."

Manuke... I'd been in Tokyo Bay often enough to know she'd just called me a 'loser'. Or a dummy.

"Hey, don't be such a *warugati*," I say. "What's your name?"

Instead of answering, she says, "Give me my keys."

Have to laugh. She's a brat alright. Chick from a Manga comic book — very popular in Japan, the style, the attitude.

I take her to the Captain. He's in his cabin, watching a flat screen monitor of the bridge, and the lst and 2nd officers taking care of business. Nonplussed when he sees the girl. He's clearly expecting his keys back. Knows Japanese too, more than me, as I don't understand a word he says to her.

"No gossiping, Mr. Caine," he says, turning to me. "This is a private matter."

"Yes, Captain."

"I mean it."

I nod, and withdraw. She smiles faintly, as if to say get lost, *manuke.*

I didn't know what he was up to, although as sure as hell I meant to find out. You can be a patsy and take the fall when the time comes or you can play the patsy and land on your feet... when the time comes.

2: Mishima

The deck hands were the usual 3rd world collection recruited on the cheap, south Asian and African and god knows what. Most looked Somali or Ethiopian to me, tall and skinny, skin like sepia and eyes that are always faraway, like they'd rather be anywhere but here. I have all their passports and tickets in the safe in my cabin and as quartermaster am supposed to know who everybody is and where they're from but you can't always trust their creds. Like I say, recruited on the cheap. The Sea Dragon was registered in Mongolia, which is a laugh because Mongolia is a landlocked nation, and the ownership group... well, who knows? Hidden within the usual maze of shell companies. For business purposes, the head office is in London, but could be just a forward answering machine. No big deal. All business is over the Internet these days anyway.

One deck guy had my attention because he was always social, greeted you with a big smile and was quick with a few words about the weather or some other bullshit. Horace Marvelous. The officers referred to him as 'Marley' because he was listed as Jamaican and acted Rasta, had dreadlocks and smoked a lot. He could sing too and had some interesting tattoos.

I was up top on the stern watching the gulls hanging in the slipstream over the ship's wake. Singapore Strait. Sunny, lots of blue and some distant piles of big white fluffy clouds. Marley came out of the elevator, broke into a big smile when he saw me.

"Horace," I say. "You look guilty."

He chuckles: "Me, boss?"

"What're you up to?"

"Checking the merch."

"All good?"

"All good, snug as a bug."

"Deck seven? The Mazdas?" We would be unloading them in Singapore.

"All good, ready to roll."

"What about Deck 13?"

He got serious. "We don't like 13, boss. We call it 14."

Normally ship decks are numbered from the bottom up but on a autoliner it was more convenient to list from the top down. Or maybe for the Sea Dragon it's an Asian thing, like the way they read from the back of the book instead of the front.

"You superstitious, Horace?"

"It pays to be on the right side of the numbers, boss."

Whatever did he mean by that? I just chuckle, pretend I'm hip.

"Well, what about 14, then? Do I need to be going down there?"

"Ballast, boss. Pure ballast."

I take this to mean the cars were sitting tight and none have shifted. We had experienced a rough patch in the South China, 42 knot side winds with a few nasty standing waves, but we sailed through, no problem. The Dragon has high walls above the water-line, so a strong wind can make things go disco and the cargo might dance. But we did o.k. and are still doing o.k. No need to think of having a drink.

"Rough seas when you left Korea, eh?"

"Cross wind."

"Too bad about Mishima."

"He was on the wrong side of the numbers."

I nod, try to figure the code.

"Accident?"

Marley smiles, says, "What else?"

"Anyone see him go overboard?"

"I believe not."

"The Tokyo cops talk to anyone?"

"Not me. Captain's business."

"Did the Captain talk to you or any of the crew? Who was on watch?"

"I cannot say, sir. I was sleeping."

"So it's a mystery...."

"Yeah, a mystery. Don't worry, boss. I see you're good on your feet. You be on the right side."

I had to hope so. I'm not superstitious but when you're filling in for a dead man, sometimes you start thinking things might repeat.

3: What Would Neeson Do?

The 3rd officer was far more accommodating. Colgan, a Belfast native, but didn't have the plebeian sing song accent. A hulking brute with a red face who looked like he belonged in the bog digging peat. Looks deceive — he had some culture, maybe a degree, and plenty of experience on the high sea.

He comes to see me in my locker room. I'm on the computer trying to figure out what fresh food requisitions Mishima had taken on in Korea but can find nada. This follows my discovery that the Hirohito Lincoln (as I now call it) wasn't logged in, is off the books. No big surprise, I guess, yet what does it mean? Stolen?

"Mr. Colgan," I say. "What can I do for you?"

"I've started smoking again," he says. "Got any Gallaghers? No, expect not. Never heard of them either, have you?"

"Afraid not," I say. "Rothman's?"

"Yeah, put it on my chit for payday."

Crew gets paid by direct deposit. I assume. Usually they settle up by credit card.

He sits down, looks at me, says in a low voice, "What sort of contract they give you?"

"The usual... why?"

"None of us have been paid."

"You're shitting me."

"The owners are winging it, man. Cash on delivery."

This isn't reassuring, although we had the cargo and it would get delivered and surely we would get paid.

"Who are the owners, Colgan?"

"I don't know for sure. Got an idea, though."

"Yeah? Let's hear it."

"The Dragon is a North Korean ghost ship."

I try not to laugh... yet, is this as crazy as it first sounds? The ship is flying a Mongolian flag.

"The ownership is NK? Mongolian flag of convenience?"

"I think so. We took on cargo in NK."

So that's why there was no port log for Korea. Colgan allows himself a little smile, reaches for his new cigs.

"May I, Quartermaster?"

"Maybe we should go on deck."

"Alrighty... wouldn't want to be starting a fire, would we?"

"No, we wouldn't."

Guess he was alluding to the fire on my last ship, the one you probably read about, big news everywhere. The Felicity Jane. Fully loaded, 8,000 cars, 3,000 of them luxury models, Bentleys and Porsches, the whole shiteroo going to the bottom of the mid Atlantic with the ship. Not my fault. When the fire broke out, I had a plan to deal with it but nobody wanted to hear it. The lst officer even went so far as to say I started it. Pissed out of your mind, he said. Fuck you, I said. In breach of the 'no smoking' rules, asshole, he said. Fuck you and the whore that licked your placenta, I said.

The fire started in the store locker, spread through the wiring. Like poison in the blood — quick, invisible, and lethal.

Later, as we stood in the sheltered enclave below the communications mast — Colgan with a cigarette, me with a mickey of Canadian Club — I learned how the Dragon docked in Wonson NK. Sea of Japan. A quick visit by night. An off-the-books hit and run, military vehicles, a violation of the UN embargo.

"Deck 13," I say.

He nods, clears his throat, sends a gob of spit over the railing.

"You been down there?" he asks.

I shake my head. No reason to — what I don't know about, I don't know about.

"Who wants this military stuff, Colgan?"

"No clue."

"Was this cooked up by the Captain and Mishima?"

"Aye, most likely. Tell you, Caine, you've landed in a den of crooks!"

I snort, say, "How about you, matey?"

He motions with his hand, says, "Give us a taste of that."

I pass him the flask and he takes a couple of hard slugs, winces with the burn.

"I'm getting out," he says. "Tomorrow, adios this cowboy."

Tomorrow we'd be in Singapore.

"Keep this to yourself," says Colgan. "You can come with me if you're smart...."

But am I smart? Maybe, but I'm also broke.

"We'll need money," says Colgan, not to me, more like he's talking to an invisible bicameral accomplice.

Long voyages can do this. Big ship, small crew, you talk to yourself lots.

He continues: "You've got cash in the safe, Caine... requisitions money. How much?"

"That's theft, man."

"Get a grip, Caine — wages owing."

He's right about that, but you know, I have to see for myself, go to the lower decks and check the cargo. I don't know Colgan well enough to trust him one way or the other. A few military trucks? Probably surplus, a bargain scoop. No big deal one way or the other.

Colgan looks at me earnestly, says, "What would Liam Neeson do?"

Liam Neeson is or was a North Irish actor, best known for some violent action movies. Big man, just like Colgan, and maybe Colgan fancies himself as Neeson. "It's not the evil you done me, mister, it's just the look of yer ugly face" blah blah, boom boom. Problem solved.

Gallow's humor. Neeson, chrissakes. I've noticed Colgan in the officer's lounge by himself playing two hands of poker at once.

"He'd kill the Captain and sink the ship, Colgan. The fascist solution is usually the best solution."

Colgan likes what he's hearing, nods, says, "You're the man I want with me."

4: Deck 13

So I go down to the lower decks, find tranche 13, open the electric door. Yellow, with black diagonal stripes, the standard Type D watertight, meaning it's kept closed during navigation but can be opened by authorized crew. I'm authorized, naturally. Whoever's on the bridge will see the indicator light, know someone's down there. And the camera will show it's me if anyone cares to check... like the Big X, say.

Down here you can hear the hum of the diesel engine sounding in the bulkheads, feel the vibration of the propeller shaft in the steel floor. The lighting is switched low for energy saving, although I don't need a flashlight to see what's what. You can smell it.

Well, there are a couple of military trucks and they're loaded with steel crates — ammunition and some other types of ordnance, looks like. But Christ Almighty, this is nothing compared to the other so-called "luxury" vehicles. Tanks, matey. Tanks.

Thirty of them. I was in the Canadian Army Reserve for a couple of years and I recognize these buggers right away — Chinese Type 59s. The 59 is a reverse engineered Soviet T-62. 100 millimeter canon, couple of turret-mount machine guns.

Old tech, sure. Surplus, maybe. But capable of inflicting serious damage, most definitely. These predators been used all over the goddamn place. Vietnam, Iraq, Iran, Sudan... Gulf War, the Indo-Pakistani War... and wars you've never heard of. 59s. Like rats, can be killed but never exterminated.

Blow me. Serious coin here, big money.

And why shouldn't I have some? Sometimes you have to roll the dice. I knew I didn't get this job because of my stellar resume... rather, I got it because it's so dodgy. I'm corruptible is what the Big X thought, and why should I disappoint the man? I got two choices: go with Colgan or go with X.

Right on cue, my walkie talkie squawks. It's X, the Captain. He wants to see me right away.

I'd kept my mouth shut about his little sex toy, if that's what she was. Still, I was damn curious about her, wondered how she fitted into the puzzle.

I hear a noise, think there's someone else down here. Spooky. I go on alert, get tight, because even if I'm familiar with the gloomy deck interiors of a large RoRo ship, there's just something, well, spooky about a basement full of shabby vintage tanks. Mild claustrophobia, most likely. Many sailors get it on these sort of vessels, especially the big tankers.

Hear it again — an eerie rustling sound, not like the soft creak and groan of all this metal as the ship makes way at its usual 15 knots.

She's been riding quite smoothly as the weather is good. But I just can't place the sound. Some of these tanks look pretty loose, like their tracks might be missing a lynch pin or two.

Another stowaway? Maybe baby... if 'My Girl From Tokyo' can be considered a stowaway. I listen some more, but the creepy vibe gets worse and I hustle on out of there.

I go to the Captain's cabin. The girl's there, looking outrageous. Short skirt, legs forever. Definitely older than I first assumed.

Ekzetera knows I'm checking her out (what man wouldn't?), allows himself a cynical smile.

"Mr. Caine." he says. "We're worried about our 3rd Officer — have you seen him?"

"Colgan? Uh, yesterday or maybe the day before."

"He's supposed to be on watch."

"Sorry, haven't seen him. I've been down below."

"Alone?"

"Colgan wasn't with me, if that's what —"

"I know, I know. Like what you see?"

"Well... perhaps. I wouldn't call a T-59 a luxury vehicle."

"What would you call it?"

"Vintage... dependable... definitely dangerous."

"Legal?"

"That's a matter of opinion, Captain."

"What do you think of the Embargo?"

"What do I think... well I think it's a business opportunity, isn't it?"

"Splendid! I told you Mr. Caine was the right man, Iris. Look at him, doesn't he look good? Got guts, too."

Iris — so that's her name. An old-fashioned handle on a brand new door. And who wouldn't want to open it?

She hands me a manila envelope, no smile, no explanation. It isn't sealed. Feels fat and soft. I take a peek — a wad of hundred dollar bills. Might add up to... well, enough for Christmas anyway.

"Signing bonus," says Ekzetera.

"Uh, what do I have to do?" I say.

"Oh nothing outside of your qualifications, Caine. When you go ashore tomorrow, you'll take Iris with you. She has some business to attend to."

I look at Iris and she has a cheeky smirk on her face. Suits me. Maybe we can get drunk together, have some fun.

"And take the 3rd Officer with you," continues Ekzetera. "If you can find him."

Usually when the quartermaster does shore excursions, he takes the ship's cook with him if it's not recreation. What the hell do we need Colgan for?

Ekzetera opens his personal safe, removes an automatic pistol, checks the clip to ensure it's full, then passes it to me.

"Make sure Iris gets back safely," he says. "Singapore can be unpredictable, despite it's reputation for law and order."

His lizard eye opens a tad, revealing the white sliver that sees nothing and everything.

"Are you nervous, Mr. Caine?"

I weigh the automatic in my hand, then stuff it behind my belt.

"Not a bit," I say. "Just wondering what we need Colgan tagging along for, is all."

"He's a big man," says Ekzetera. "Could be useful. Anyway, don't worry — Iris will fill you in."

The eye closes. Iris smiles. I nod, leave.

5: The Poseidon Group

Ever been to Singapore? That's where they whip offenders in public and have a boat on top of three sky scrappers. Not a real boat of course, just an architectural folly. They say there's a great bar and restaurant there, 52 floors up, I think, although I've never been. I've always stayed close to the dock. Most of the dives are gone now, replaced by the yuppy style, more for tourists and the smooth operators from the SGX. City state, you'd call it. Very clean, lots of high towers and parks but they do have a few vagrants in the shadows, despite the propaganda. It's not big. Mostly an island, South China Sea on one side, the Indian Ocean on the other. You could ride your polo pony around it in a day and a night if you didn't dawdle to admire the birds.

It's a splendid looking place these days, top 10 *Forbes* for doing business, 35 billionaires and probably more they don't know about. After the war and the exit of Japan, Britain passed the colony on to Malaya. That didn't last long — one year, two years? Nasty ethnic squabbles and so Singapore went indie and now it's the biggest port in the world. Well, maybe Rotterdam is bigger, or New York, but believe me, the Port of Singapore is big.

So it's not new to me, although driving through the city in a vintage Lincoln fitted with diplomatic plates which may or may not be legit is. When we linger at the traffic intersections, we get lots of looks.

You don't want to know stuff about my childhood or wives one and two. Cut to the chase, Caine. Give them the juice, and the blood if it comes to that. Will do, am doing. As we all know, self-abuse is a short-cut to genius. That's why I drink, that's why I drink and drive, like I'm driving now through downtown Singapore with a hot little Tokyo bird who's telling me where to go, seems to be the boss of this whole shady business, whatever it really is.

Colgan's in the back seat. He's wearing a jacket and his old school tie, could pass for a diplomat riding with his security and his secretary, although of course he doesn't look Asian and this Lincoln belongs in the old movies. He's wearing sunglasses, though, and that gives him some Hollywood appeal. Movies. That's what I told them at the Terminal security gate when I handed in our passports for inspection: we're making a movie, just on our way to the location. A look at Iris was all the proof they needed... and Colgan, who could pass for Neeson, is bonus.

Colgan can't believe his good luck, of course.

When the Captain sent me looking for him, it took me a while to figure out where he was hiding. It was Marley who told me where to look, said he'd seen the 3rd Officer messing around the ship-to-shore cutter that we keep stashed on the starboard side. I check and sure enough, he's in there, lying across the moulded plastic seats. First, I think he's pissed because there's a liquor bottle lying nearby. He's out of it but still ticking. He's staged this, trying to get himself cashiered, I think. But what about that gash on the side of his head? Clown clipped a bulkhead or fell and hit himself on something. Didn't occur to me that someone had attacked him, stuffed him in there.

"Caine," he groaned. "They're onto me."

"You're up shit creek, Colgan," I said. "You missed your watch."

"I don't care... somebody bushwhacked me, christ...."

"Yeah... a bottle of Black Bush, looks like. Idiot."

And so on. Marley and me got him out of there, took him to medical, got him fixed up. True enough, the wound looked like he'd been whacked by someone with something ugly, like a machete. Or possibly a bottle, but hey, I'm no detective.

Before he went back to his duties, Marley winked at me, tapped the side of his head. Yeah, read you, man. The 3rd Officer is loco.

Amazing how quickly Colgan was able to shake his mishap off. Couple of stitches, a cup of tea, a fag and again he was whispering about how he had to escape the Sea Dragon. He blamed the 1st Officer for the "attack" — Viktor Rublev, the Russian from St. Petersburg. The other officers called him Vic when being social in the lounge. Crew called him 'Putin' behind his back because he was a bit of a martinet, played bad cop as the Big X preferred to hang back, assume the mythical role. Standard shit. Life is ugly but it's not god's fault.

"You see him?" I said.

"He hates my guts," said Colgan. "Hates the British."

This was possible. There was a chill between Moscow and London. But enough to propel Rublev to try and murder Colgan?

"But did you see him, Colgan?"

"How could I? Don't have eyes in the back of my head, do I?"

"Ship rolled, you lost your footing, smacked your head."

"Aye? How'd I wake up inside the cutter? Tell me that, Caine."

I couldn't, except he reeked of booze... and there was a bottle.

"I'm not a good scout, Caine. They know that."

"Maybe so, Colgan. But listen to me — here's your chance to reform...."

I told him about the mission the Big X had assigned us for the next day. He was suspicious but was willing to go along. I suppose he was thinking he could break cover when he got ashore if he didn't like the game. I liked Colgan. Wanted to help him. His scruples seemed naive, a sort stupidity we all pass through before seeing the light. And you don't build up your pension fund by being stupid, do you?

We're on a open stretch, not far from the Embassy district. I'm getting used to the heavy steering of this old timer.

"No father, eh," I say to Iris.

"What are you talking about?" she says sharply. "Eyes on the road. Take the next left."

I wait until I finish the turn, then say, "You and the Captain, Iris."

"What are you talking about, manuke?"

"You and the Big X," I say. "Pure Freud. Isn't that right, Mr. Colgan? Iris has a daddy complex."

"I don't care," says Colgan hoarsely. "Are we stopping soon? I need a drink."

"You guys are crybabies," says Iris. "Mind on the business, please."

"If only I knew what the business is," says Colgan.

"You know," I say. "Iris is meeting with the buyer. Right, Iris?"

"Go down here," says Iris. "Keep going... it's a hidden driveway."

The road sign says 'Mandalay'. Upscale neighbourhood. Fancy houses with fancy gardens. Some even have gatehouses. Traffic sparse — no trucks and no peasant three wheeler vans around here.

"Big money," I say. "These guys don't pay tax."

"Mr. Caine," says Iris. "Please keep your thoughts to yourself. The stake that sticks up gets hammered down."

I chuckle, say, "Hear that, Colgan? Be silent, be dumb. Not knowing is Buddha."

Iris scowls.

"Pull over," says Iris. "Do it, Caine."

I coast to a stop by the kerb. Can see Number 11, next gateway ahead. Later learn the Japanese requisitioned the property for the Imperial Army HQ when they captured Singa from the British. Nice digs for the Rising Sun.

"Smart remarks are inappropriate," says Iris. "You must be professional, alert."

"Fair enough," I say. "But will I be expected to kill anyone?"

"Don't be ridiculous. I have to meet someone. Won't take long."

"What are we supposed to do?"

"Look ugly — you can do that, can't you?"

"Sure — Colgan's a natural."

Colgan takes exception to this.

"This is outside my job description," he says. "This is beyond overtime. And I need a piss."

Iris is bristling.

"Chill," I say to Colgan. "You'll get paid bonus."

"Wouldn't that be nice," says Colgan. "To actually get paid."

"Let's go," says Iris. "We're late already."

The house is concealed by the garden, which is pretty lush and obviously well tended, even the idols that sit near the pond, some partially concealed in the bushes. I don't know much about architecture but this place looks big money to me. Straight line modern with some Asian curves. The big windows on either side of the double front door shine like a nice pair of sunglasses — mysterious and very cool.

Half-dozen cars parked on the paved concourse near the wide front steps. Top models, all bright and clean like they just came from the showroom.

Colgan relieves himself behind a small folly with a golden Buddha inside.

"What is this place?" I say to Iris.

"Private club," she says.

This could mean anything. Place is awfully quiet.

Inside is a mess. Well, I underrate it — it's a wreck, like somebody exchanged cigarettes with the devil.

Reeks. Ammonium nitrate, for sure. Harsh. I've inhaled a few ugly smells, seen a few ugly sights — in Afghanistan, for one — but nothing quite like this, maybe because the place is so upscale and is now a smoldering ruin littered with, um, smoldering bodies flung here and there, arranged like the card table just exploded in a grotesque mandala. Strangely, the big table is still fairly intact. Some of them were shot, maybe for insurance. Don't count them, because some are just pieces. Bus boys too, their white tunics splattered with blood and shit. The business men... well, they don't look like much more of anything than roadkill.

One guy is hanging from the ceiling, like a bat that got hung up in the trees. Those aren't wings, I realize. Stretched, shredded skin. A strange, grotesque crucifixion.

Enough to make you throw up, which is exactly what Colgan does. Iris moves close to me — real close.

My hand is on the automatic stuck behind my belt. Draw it out slowly as my eyes roam the surround. Scene looks fresh, the devil could still be here, lurking in one of the corridors, or behind that oriental tapestry that somehow survived the carnage. Pic of a serpentine red dragon. Probably worth big bucks.

"Guess the deal is off," I murmur.

Iris is gripping my arm as she scans the faces that can be scanned. Malays, looks like. Asian anyway.

Colgan's trying to pull himself together.

"I want to go home," he says, feebly, just like a child.

"Get a grip," I say to him. "Go and wait in the car."

A man appears behind us. Tall guy, white suit, just like some dude who owns a plantation and keeps a mistress in town. Asian... could be Malay or Mongolian or anything in between, maybe Eurasian for that matter. Skin so smooth he never has to shave.

He's smiling without showing teeth. Looks superb and knows it.

"Iris," he says. "What's the shortest distance between two lines?"

He's juggling a hand grenade. No answer required.

Iris points at the bodies, barks, "What is this?"

The handsome man shrugs, says, "Picasso?"

Very funny. Guess he thinks he's a stage designer or something.

"All of them? This is big mistake."

Here they break into Japanese, although you don't need to know any to get the drift. She calls him 'Dazai', I think. It's in the scramble. And what is he to her? More than a money mule, methinks. Too much heat, too much frisson. Mind you, when there's a dude with a grenade and the room is full of bodies and what's left of the house is as silent as a bloody grave, which it is, your head can get a bit irrational because the distance between life and death gets very short.

He's looking at me and Colgan, who's frozen in a sort of half-turn, too freaked to move.

"And who are these detectives?"

"From the Dragon, idiot. Stop messing with that bomb, o.k."

He nods, pockets the grenade in the side pocket of his loose jacket which I now notice has a red smear.

"Put the gun away," Iris says to me.

I obey, but not before giving the man a hard, don't-fuck-with-me stare.

"This one," he says, meaning me. "Your new boyfriend?"

"This is Caine," she says. "He drives my car."

"Is that all, Iris? He looks, er, capable."

"He is capable. He's the quartermaster."

His eyes narrow in sudden recognition: "I know this man — he sank the Felicity Jane!"

I've had enough. Fuck this playboy and the mother who set him loose.

"Who says?" I say.

"I say," he says. "Insured by the Poseidon Group."

"So what? What's your business?" I say.

"Export," says Iris.

"I can see that," I say, gesturing towards the bodies. "What else?"

"Collections," he says.

His eyelids go to half-shutter as the Buddha smile crosses his handsome face. He's Korean, I think.

He takes the grenade from his pocket, tosses it to me. Bloody hell!

"Good reaction," he says.

"I don't need it," I say.

The grenade feels hot even though it isn't. Must be from his hand but gotta say, he looks cool.

"Give it to the Buddha," he says.

"I will," I say. "And who are these guys?"

His eyes drift sideways for a second.

"Behold," he says. "The Poseidon Group."

He's talking about the bodies, the dead platoon, the bits and pieces.

We go outside and I toss the grenade into the pond near the Buddha shrine. Don't pull the pin, of course.

The Poseidon Group. Very glad we arrived late.

It's all very interesting. And it gets more interesting because, not only did these unfortunate businessmen take the bite for the Felicity Jane sinking, they also had money in the Sea Dragon, particularly the "luxury vehicle" part of its cargo. It all comes out in the return drive to the dock, Dazai in the back instead of Colgan.

And where's Colgan? He's in the trunk. Didn't want to comply, of course, especially as he had to swap clothes with Dazai (so we would look the same going back as going out) and he's a big guy and no big guy likes getting into the trunk, even if it is big and roomy, like this Hirohito Lincoln trunk.

"Do it, Neeson," I said. "I've got your back."

"Drop me off at the nearest tavern," he said. "Let me get drunk."

Such a romantic, and not really clued as to his options, which, in reality, were only two. One, Mr. Dazai wanted him on board and wouldn't take no for an answer, and two, the Mazdas had been off-loaded and the Sea Dragon would sail with the tide... as the Big X had made perfectly clear before we left on our mission.

6: Iris

Iris got attacked. Had to happen. She couldn't expect to creep around the ship with impunity, especially with at least 20 sex-starved swabbies going about their lonely business on a boat this big. Guess she was checking her car. Helped with home-sickness... or at least that's my theory. We weren't set for a rendezvous.

But as it happened, I was in the Zil which was parked a couple of slots away from the Lincoln, lying on my back, head stuck under the dash, checking just in case this baby was wired with something unpleasant. Long shot, wasn't expecting it to be, but you never know, might have been an unauthorized upgrade. Zils are made in Moscow and the company is in the armaments business too, artillery shells and military vehicles. But I couldn't spot anything untoward, it all looked stock.

I'd talked to 1st Office Rublev about the Zil, assumed he'd know something about this Soviet dinosaur, but he was disinterested, said if he needed a car, he'd get a BMW.

So I was there, just snooping around, and it was a lucky thing for her I was because who knows where it might've ended. Assault, then a Mishima moment, maybe.

I was just straightening up when I heard her muffled scream. Had to be her, as she's the only woman on board. Zil windows are tinted, so I had to open the door or lower the window, make some noise either way. The key was in the ignition, so I was able to power down the window see what was going on in the shadowy car deck. Discreetly.

There's a struggle going on between her and some guy over by the stairs, not far from the Lincoln. He's got her in a choke and is pushing her forward, like he wants to get her bent over and face down on the hood of the nearest car. Simple sexual assault, seen it a million times in the parking lots of any seaport city you care to name. Luckily I have the automatic the Big X gave me, although I'm thinking, why don't I just watch for a while... this might not be what I think it is.

Guy's big, swears in broken English. When he gets her positioned, he rips down her jeans exposing her shapely art gallery ass. Oh hum, guess I have to step in... and I do. He's just unzipped himself when I come up behind him, give him chop with my gun, enough to give him concussion and bad movies for a month. He gasps, releases Iris, rolls to one side, doesn't hit the deck because I grab his belt with my free hand. He's not quite out although his eyes are rolling. Don't recognize him. One of the East Africans or maybe an Arab. A blender, know what I mean? Skin is light enough to pass for anything, especially wearing a suit, although this bastard isn't dressed for the office as his suit is a survival suit like he'd just been outside doing a hull inspection.

Everything happens quickly. Iris swivels, and christ, she's got a small knife that she drives into the guy's gut — one, twice, fast, like it's something she's done before.

I let go, and he drops.

"Pig," hisses Iris.

She pulls up her jeans. Meanwhile the guy's eyes relax into marble.

"That was excessive, baby," I say.

"Pig," she says again.

"I had him on ice, fer chrissakes. I'm sure the Cap would've liked to ask him some questions."

Iris looks him over. Roadkill. Unfortunate business but there you go.

"Know him?" I ask.

"He cleans my cabin. Pig."

Interesting. Nobody cleans for me or makes my bed... but then I'm not a woman.

"Well, Iris, what now?"

"Don't tell Zee."

"He tried to rape you."

"So? Then he got what he deserve. I will not be humiliated."

She has a point. Technically it's self-defense, although if there were any detectives around and this went to court, it could be made into murder. Mind you, here, on the high seas, the Captain would be the judge and jury and somehow I think our Captain wouldn't want this going public. I know what has to be done, but I want to hear her say it.

"Well, you weren't humiliated, but you have a problem."

"We have a problem."

She emphasizes the "we", right?

"I didn't kill him, baby," I say.

"You hit him pretty hard," she says.

Fortunately there's no one around to hear any of this or witness what's going down.

"Let's not fight," she says. "We hide him in the trunk."

The good old trunk. But that's only good for a little while for obvious reasons. We're days away from any vehicle disembarkation.

We put the body in the Bentley — it's one of the newer ones — and that night we use a dolly, get him up on deck, and heave him over the side. He drops like a dagger. His upturned face and mouth are frozen in a snarl, like his dick is still stiff and ready. Will he be missed?

Will one of his buddies stop off at the Quartermaster's crib, start bitching? Will the Captain give a shit? I think not.

Hope she's grateful. I saved her ass, maybe her life.

7: The Big X and the Hirohito Lincoln

The Indian Ocean — lots of people and vessels go missing there. Boats, aircraft, UFOs, space stations... the southern region is used as a dump for space junk, goes by the romantic name 'Point Nemo' on the charts, although the technical name is the 'Oceanic Pole of Inaccessibility' because it's considered the world's most remote spot. Deep. A long way from anywhere so when you're heading for the Horn or East Africa or the Arabian Peninsula and the Gulf, you're skirting it. I thought we were heading for Mumbai as that's what my computer said and the Big X said he was dying for some Indian food.

All nonsense, of course. India doesn't need any T-59 tanks.

Sea gets pretty rough and I get ansty. Iris too. She's taken to visiting me in one of the several cars still parked on Deck 1. A three year old Bentley, the sort narcos everywhere prefer. She wants privacy, but for what reason? The ship is groaning as it rolls and shudders. Not too bad, as the Dragon has decent stabilizers. But all this metal and all these cars just wanna moan.

I would've preferred the traditional luxury of the Hirohito Lincoln but she says that's the first place "they" would look.

She's still calling me '*manuke*' but a little more tenderly. Things aren't as sweet between her and the Big X ever since Mr. Dazai joined us, it seems.

"Dazai wants to change course, offload someplace else. Different buyer or something."

"What does the Captain think?"

"Doesn't want to."

This could be a problem, I think. Two Captains.

Is this all she wants to tell me? She seems to be running away from something or someone. Had this feeling from the first day I found her in the car.

She's looking for a confessor. No surprise considering what's been going down.

"My mother has a hotel," she says. "It was a kiss-off from her lover, Prince Goro."

Goro — some sort of descendant of Emperor Hirohito. Playboy grandson, maybe.

"The car, too?"

"Yeah. He gave her the car. Said it was worth more than the hotel."

"Where's the hotel?"

"Yoko. It's not much. Three star. Baishunfu and sailors use it. Some tourists. I worked on the desk after I dropped out of uni."

"How old are you?"

"Old enough. Why?"

"You and the Captain — I don't get it."

"He stayed at the hotel between voyages. He liked the whores."

Ekzetera — the Big X — was turning out to be quite the gigolo. Hard to believe. He was 60 if he was a day one way or the other. Had to be shooting blanks if he was shooting at all.

Iris? Daughter like mother, it seems. Got it, use it. Mom was running a geisha game, service of the hotel.

I knew I'd be a fool to underestimate Iris, no matter how friendly she got.

"Tell me about the Felicity Jane," she says.

"No thanks," I say. "I just did a year in therapy because of Jane."

"You're funny, manuke. What was the real cargo? Come on, don't be shy."

"Cars, baby. It was all legit."

"I don't believe it. Dazai says you were hired to sink the ship."

"Dazai's got a big mouth. Who is he anyway... besides being a homicidal maniac? An enforcer for the real seller of the tanks?"

Meaning the NK government... NK, always strapped for cash to fund its weapons program and keep the glorious leader and the party elite flush in pocket money.

"He's a weapons dealer... you know that."

"Uh huh... so he's the real Big X."

"Dazai is... well, he's a poet."

Now it's her turn to be funny. I hiss.

"Yes," says Iris. "He won a prize in uni for his poetry. You like poetry?"

"Aw yeah. Read some every night before I fall asleep."

"Dazai is the master of the suicide haiku."

My mind flashes to the shredded bodies of the Poseidon Group: yeah, you could call that a haiku... if you didn't count the syllables.

Maybe a koan, if you recall any Zen. A conundrum.

"What university?"

"Tokyo. Lots of foreign students."

"I thought Koreans hated Japanese."

"Not so much. Money talks, you know."

"I hope you and Dazai haven't got a suicide pact going. There's a lot of ammunition and god knows what else in those trucks in the hold."

"Ammunition? Not much. Just demo, a few rounds. Didn't you look?"

Fact is, I didn't actually. I assumed these crates and steel boxes were all holding ordnance, enough to make this sleeping battalion ready to rock.

"So what do you expect me to do, princess?" I say. "You're not leaving the dark side just to tease me, right?"

She put a hand on top of mine. Warm. Could feel her nails as it tightened.

"Be ready," she says.

I'm as ready as I'll ever be on the edge of a storm in the Indian Ocean. Mumbai or, hmm, is it Dubai? They rhyme and sometimes I get them confused. We're supposed to be going to one of them to drop off the remaining autos but now, with Dazai in the picture, who knows the real destination?

I find it's better not to ask too many questions, because questions reveal what you know just as easily as what you don't know. Like the poet says, dogs bark, the moon remains full, and the clouds are full of light.

8: Blackjack

Word gets around. Everybody knew there was a woman on board and everybody figured she was the Big X's trophy or if she wasn't that, she was connected to Dazai somehow. A mistress maybe. As Dazai didn't eat dinner with the officers — well, he didn't eat much, and what he did eat, he ate alone in his cabin — and socialize, they regarded him as the owner of the Sea Dragon.

Possibly he was just the titular owner for some company run by the bosses in Pyongyang but when it came to the cargo and its disposal, he would be the man.

He was the real replacement for Mishima, who was just an NK stooge put on board to keep an eye on Ekzetera, and Ekzetera had him offed.

Colgan's theory, not mine.

"He do it himself?" I say. "Captain's pretty small."

"Maybe Rublev helped him," says Colgan.

"You've got it in for Rublev, haven't you?"

"Just tryin' to connect the dots, mister. Something's not right here."

Obviously... yet surely Colgan knew this when he signed on. My feeling was Colgan was testing me, trying to get me to reveal something

I shouldn't legitimately know.

Same with Marley. For instance, the time I went looking for him to ask if the crew was all present and accounted for. He was in the crew lounge, 3rd deck, playing his guitar. Not bad. Said he used to gig on the Mayan Riviera. Probably true and probably the only true thing he said that day.

"No, boss," he said. "Nobody missing."

"Isn't there a steward who cleans cabins?"

He laughed.

"That's crazy, man. We ain't no cruise ship."

I changed tack.

"Seen the woman?"

He nodded, still smiling big and friendly. Except that

jailhouse tattoo on his neck made him look a little less trustworthy, unless you thought it was hip and Rasta Man was all show biz.

"Very nice," he said, and played the riff from Deep Purple's 'My Woman From Tokyo'. "Your secret's safe with me."

"What do you mean by that, Horace?"

"Be cool, man. Just joking. She's *primo*, that's all."

"You talk to her?"

"Alas, no. Captain wouldn't like it."

"Put his evil eye on you, eh?"

"That is correct, Mr. Caine. The Captain see everything. He has cameras in secret places."

Well, I didn't know how secret they were, although the ship CCTV was state of the art.

"Tell me, Horace, you been down on Deck 13 recently?"

"No, boss. I never go there."

"You sure? I thought I heard you singing when I was checking the cargo."

"Not I, sir. Maybe you hear music in the iron."

"Music in the iron — what's that?"

"Ship music, man. Ship got the blues, dig?"

The ship did have a sound, right enough. All ships do. Engine noise, bulkhead creak, hull vibration. Some folks like it, others get creeped. I'm used to it, although what I heard of Deck 13 wasn't music in the iron.

"You got something on your mind, boss?"

"Could we have a stowaway in one of those, er, 'luxury' vehicles?"

"Another lady?"

"Sure. Or maybe some guy who saw his chance to defect when the Dragon loaded in Wonsan."

"Korea all look the same to me, man."

"Right. Not knowing is Buddha."

"I see you are a wise man. Hey, you should check those funeral chariots, Mr. Quartermaster man. You have suspicions, you check them. Two women better than one."

"Very funny, Horace. I'll stick with 'music in the iron', I think."

Then Iris decided to put in a social appearance with the crew. When I say 'crew', I mean the officers. Said she was bored, needed to have some fun. Bit of an insult really as I thought she was having plenty of fun in those fabulous cars with yours truly. Don't know what Ekzetera thought of her plan, as I know he thought it was better she stay private, well away from the hungry eyes of the unbaptised crew. Yet... possibly he put her up to it as a way of goading Dazai, showing him who was boss and that Iris was his to do with what he wished.

As for myself, it was sweet playing patsy... but for how long? For now, I'd be the obedient little mule.

I gave the automatic back to Ekzetera. He ejected the clip, checked the ammo.

"You didn't use it, Mr. Caine," he said. "I like that. Discipline."

Truth was, I had fired it a few times into the ocean when the wind noise was high and nobody was around, just to see how it felt, and it felt good. Had some extra ammo too. Deck 13 supplies.

"Gunfire wakes the neighbours," I said.

"It can, it can. Is this the same gun I gave you? Feels different somehow."

"Where would I get another?"

"Hmm... it's a Hamada Type 1, you know."

"Japanese?"

"Yes. Essentially a copy of the 1910 Browning."

"Japs make good copies."

The lizard orb opened slightly, surveyed me shrewdly.

"Yes they do. But tell me, sir, when does a copy cease to be a copy?"

"You mean like wife number 2?"

He chuckled. "You're astute, Mr. Caine. Yes, like wife number 2."

"If I knew the answer to that, Captain, I wouldn't be here."

I knew he was signalling Iris. I knew he was saying don't think I don't know, Quartermaster. She's a reward for services rendered, that's all. And don't be thinking otherwise. Yeah, I knew what he language he was speaking. He was the Big X and liked to talk in analogues. He didn't care a double 'F' for this pistol or that pistol.

Suits me. When it comes to women, I've learned my lesson.

Blackjack, that's what she had in mind. A little evening of 21 to strip the guys of their high seas tension and make them pussy cats for the new agenda, whatever it was shaping up to be. By and large they behaved themselves. They played regular poker for a couple hours, then the lady showed up with Ekzetera. 3rd Officer Colgan was in the bridge.

Frankly, poker bores the ass of me. I just watched, drank a little rum in my coffee. I was starting to feel pissed off, either because of Iris or because of Ekzetera. The Cap was playing me on a string. How many of these crises were engineered by him? Paranoid tests of loyalty or bluffs to stage his agenda, whatever it was. Passing the tanks to a buyer, sure, but to the same buyer Dazai had contracted? And would any of us share in the money as promised?

9: Ping Pong

Turns out, Dazai considers himself a ping pong ace. There's a table set up in the crew lounge and once in a while somebody has a go.

I was there getting myself a sandwich from the buffet when I see him playing the 2nd Officer, Jurgens, who's German although moves around with a Danish passport. Why? Maybe he has a Danish wife or maybe he bought it on the black market. The photo shows a stone-faced Nazi if ever there was one — a skull with blue eyes and thin, twisted lips — although the few words I've exchanged with him have been friendly. Despite what the passport photo shows, he can smile, and when at sea, he lets his blond hair get long. Maybe once upon a time he was a rocker, got busted for something, had to get out of Berlin on a barge heading for the Baltic.

He's an o.k. table tennis player. Better than me. What I notice are his hands. Seem a little bigger.

Both these guys stand way back from the table as they're hitting hard, exchanging *Petushkas*. Jurgens snarls with each stroke, Dazai hisses. These guys can rally too.

Seems they're betting on the match. When Jurgens wins a fistful of paper, Dazai demands another game. The only reason he lost was because his left shoe lace broke and he lost his balance. I saw it happen. Maybe so, but this man lost his balance way before any of this.

The occasional roll of the ship doesn't make it any easier either.

It's funny, though. I wonder if Jurgens has any idea what he's up against. Dazai doesn't like to lose.

"That's it," says Jurgens. "You want to play more, play Caine."

"A rematch," says Dazai. "You saw what happened."

"So? Wear boots next time."

"The honourable thing is to replay the game."

"You want your money back? Forget it."

"I'm not asking for you to give it back, Officer Jurgens. I'm asking for a chance to win it back."

Jurgens glances my way, smiles, then comes over, offers me the paddle.

"Uh uh," I say. "I got a sandwich to eat."

"I want you," says Dazai, giving Jurgens the lock stare. "Rematch."

Jurgens holds out the money he just won. "Take this," he says. "I'll spot you."

"Fatal mistake," I say. "I'm no good."

"He's easy, man — you can take him."

Dazai doesn't like jokes and definitely not teasing... and somehow I feel Jurgens isn't really teasing, is just winding the man up.

It's here that Colgan arrives, announces that he loves ping pong, can he get a game?

"We play for money, Colgan," says Jurgens. "Hundred American per game, o.k.?"

Colgan looks doubtful, rubs his chin like he missed a few hairs when shaving. He has that look about him. Scruffy, just a few steps from sleeping on a park bench.

"I didn't know you could play, Jurgens," he says. "Maybe you're good."

"I am," says Jurgens. "But you can play Mr. Dazai and I'll play the winner."

"You ever played?" I say to Colgan.

"Been a while," he says. "What say we play some warm-up?"

"I'm already warm," says Dazai. "Show me money or go away."

On this ship, nobody's walking around with money in his pocket. Dazai and Jurgens seem to be the exceptions. But I'm quartermaster, can cover the float, dock it from pay day. So I bank Colgan, the big fool, let him have at it.

And what a surprise, especially for Dazai who figured he could wipe Colgan off the face of the planet with a couple of his nuclear strikes.

Yeah, Colgan loses the first game, but he smokes Dazai

in next two, takes the match. Dazai is choked and I figure he's going to smash his paddle either on the bulkhead or Colgan's faintly smug face. We'd all underestimated the man. Guess we shouldn't have made him ride in the trunk of the Lincoln.

"You are very agile," says Dazai.

I notice he doesn't pant, although his voice is tight.

No smile, no good loser.

"A hundred Uncle Sams," says Colgan, holding out a big red hand.

His fingers wiggle, like a crab left on the beach in the roll of the surf.

"I pay you later," says Dazai.

"What gobshite is this?" exclaims Colgan. "Didn't he say 'show me the money or bugger off'?'"

"Relax, Colgan," I say. "He'll pay. Guy's loaded."

Colgan looks at Dazai, then at me, says, "The man didn't put up his ante, did he?"

Blah blah, on it goes. 2nd Officer Jurgens, who watched this fiasco in self-disgust, says he'll concede his match, offers the hundred he won from Dazai to Colgan but Colgan waves it off. The big man is acting like a big man, seems to be itching for a fight. He moves in close to Dazai, is almost bumping chests. I wonder if Colgan has had a drop. Don't smell it and he certainly isn't moving like a guy who's slipped out of first gear.

I'm wondering if all his previous anxiety fits were just an act. Maybe he's bi-polar.

There's a helluva roar suddenly. A jet or something, making a low level pass. This breaks up the party, gets us outside onto the deck scanning the cloudy marbled sky. Away from the air conditioning, it's humid, even with the 15 knot wind that's ruffling the waves. I see Marley and he's pointing. I see it, moving fast towards the horizon like a black dart. It banks, then returns, passing us off starboard a half kilometer before turning west and disappearing into the marine murk where the sky meets the ocean.

"A B-2 stealth bomber," I say to no one in particular.

"What does he want?" says Colgan.

"Just saying *hallo*," says Jurgens, using the German.

"Where's he from?" says Colgan.

"Diego Garcia," I say. "Should think."

"Fantasy Island," says Colgan. "Ever been there?"

I play dumb. I've been everywhere and nowhere, right? Depends on the occasion.

The Americans and the Brits have a base there, just south of the equator, mid-Indian. Chagos Archipelago. We aren't that far away, maybe 800 kilometers more or less. Nothing for a B-2 'flying wing'. Nothing for a hi-tech bat looking for some target practice on a big lumbering RoRo carrier heading… well, where were we heading? I look towards the bridge, see lst Officer Rublev on the outside gangway scanning the distance with binoculars. The Captain joins him, takes the nocs, also has a look.

Marley sidles up, says to me, "Bad karma, boss."

I'm not sure what he's referring to — the flyby or Dazai, who's standing by himself, stone faced and half-shuttered eyes like he's picking up signals from outer space.

10: Moonlight

I find Captain Ekzetera in the Hirohito Lincoln, his hands gripping the steering wheel, eyes locked on some imaginary highway. Iris is in the back, looking hot and ready for a magazine cover. Red lipstick lips, black pencil eyes, some blush, smelling great, and wearing a black silk kimono suit — tunic top, pants — with trad Japanese red buttons and the rays of the rising sun. It's like they're heading for a reception in Nagasaki before the bomb drops... know what I'm saying? Fake happy, reeking of doom.

I get in, sit in the front passenger seat. Leather. Sprung soft, like an old mattress.

"I love this car, Mr. Caine," says Ekzetera softly. "It rides the road like a ship rides the sea."

"You got that right," I say. "This baby floats."

"Iris used to drive me to the Shinto Temple at O. The Temple of the Two Moons. Very relaxing. Ever been there? No? You wouldn't know The Seven Gods of Fortune, then, would you...."

"I've heard of them."

"I used to pray there — this surprises you, I can see. Yes, I have spiritual side."

I grunt, say, "So what did you pray for? Money?"

Ekzetera laughs politely, says, "Well yes, naturally. Success in business."

"It work for you?"

"In the past, yes. Recently...."

He trails off. Lost his mojo, no doubt. Dazai, the suicide poet, no doubt.

Iris had told me previously that Ekzetera had asked her to have the car blessed for purification. They drove through a car wash close to the temple. Priests probably were silent partners.

"To business," he resumes. "It might be necessary to sink the ship."

Can't be insurance, I think. The Poseidon Group is kaput.

"Can you do that, Mr. Caine?"

"Captain, you could do it."

"Not with a bang."

He's alluding to the Felicity Jane. I might as well come clean. The luxury cars on the Jane were part of a terrorist plot. All wired with 'Moonlight', an ingenious and deadly explosive concealed within the technology of the autos. Each one, when detonated, had the equivalent force of 10k C 4 plastic. That's big, people. That beats your average Beruit truck bomb by 4 fold. You wanna take out an airport passenger terminal or bring down a modest commercial highrise in Manhattan? Use Moonlight. The happy owner of his new Bentley or Porsche would have no clue, just deliver the hidden message during the normal course of his perambulation. The explosive would be detonated by an terrorist operative using a cell phone and an individual code for the specific car. Imagine the devastation and chaos that 500 cars dispersed to the ruling classes of the USA would've caused, the terror and complete enigma of it all. It was a cozy little plan for sure.

And no dog can sniff Moonlight. A thin wire between being and nothingness.

So I had to sink the Felicity Jane, make it look like an unfortunate accident. No point in revealing your intel to the bogies. Play dumb, let them try again, reveal themselves... hunt 'em down.

"We're not heading for the Horn or the Arabian Peninsula, are we?"

"No, Caine, we're not. Our destination is the Bombal Channel."

The Bombal Channel... this is in the Chagos Archipelago, the group of atolls where Diego Garcia is located. An unwise port of call for a ship carrying 30 North Korean surplus tanks, you'd think. Mind you, there are 60 islands in the group, many with lush tropical jungle, so you might be able to creep in there if you stay far enough away from Diego Garcia and make like you're just passing through.

"The customer for the luxury vehicles is there?" I say.

"Yes," says Ekzetera. "We all want to get paid."

"What's the problem, then?"

Of course I could think of several problems. The Chagos were crawling with Americans with all kinds of deadly force, and as far as I knew, all the islanders had been kicked out to make way for the base. While everyone knew about the airbase and the deep space satellite tracking station, a little more off the radar was the CIA rendition prison where all sorts of bad stuff was going on in the name of goodness. And there were problems with the islanders, the Chagos. Not all of them liked American dollars and British pounds and living someplace else. They wanted to come back, reclaim Fantasy Island.

"The problem is Mr. Dazai," says Ekzetera.

No surprise.

"Is he RGB?"

"Unofficially, I'm sure."

RGB is the North Korean intel unit. Short for 'Reconnaissance General Bureau'. They perform the usual tricks.

"Where does he want to go?"

"South."

"South? There's nothing there!"

"He thinks there is."

"Tell him to take a hike — you're the Captain, aren't you?"

"Clap him in irons, should I?"

"I would."

Ekzetera sighs, says, "He has friends on board."

Now why do I think of Iris? She's being awfully quiet, relaxing like a pussy cat in the big back seat. But he's not talking about Iris.

"You got names?" I ask.

"I don't," says Ekzetera. "It might be too late to find out anyway."

"There's gotta be more than money in this for you, Captain."

Now Iris speaks: "The Captain's mother was from Chagos,

manuke. Creole Malay. In a way, it's his homeland, even if he wasn't born here."

"Touching," I say. "Why don't I believe it?"

"You don't have to help us," says Iris.

"Yeah? What's your cut, geisha girl?"

"Same as yours... cash on delivery."

I'm wondering how they planned on off-loading 30 tanks in the Bombal Channel. Ekzetera fills me in on that. The Chagos invasion group have acquired a flat deck log carrier. Low profile, easy off-load. Plenty of parking space. Night gig. Collect the money and sail on.

And what is Dazai's problem with this?

"He speaks in riddles," says Ekzetera. "As you know, he's a very dangerous man."

"Don't seem that dangerous to me," I say. "No weapon, no problem."

"It's the crew that's the problem."

I shrug, say, "Lend me your gun again and I'll see what I can do."

"A gunfight might not settle anything."

"You want my help or not?"

Ekzetera sighs again, then pulls an automatic from his jacket, passes it to me.

"Keep it," he says. "I have another."

Iris?"

Iris scowls, says, "I hate guns."

I open the door, but before I get out, I have a couple more questions.

"Are we on course for the Chagos?"

The Captain nods.

"Who's on the bridge?"

"2nd Officer Jurgens."

"The wheel?"

"Seaman Marley."

"So all normal."

"For now, yes."

"That flyby mean anything?"

"Normal behaviour around here."

Normal behaviour, eh. I wonder. I hate getting squeezed between two agendas. And for all I could tell, there might even be other players, other games. The politics of this autoliner were crazier than a cruise ship full of drunk seniors.

As I exit the Lincoln and close the door, I look at Iris through the closed window. She smiles faintly. She knows what I want... and maybe later I will.

II: Suckered

I should've been on guard but I wasn't. I had the Captain's gun but y'know, two days passed and we were nearly at the archipelago and everything was looking peachy normal. I was fact checking some of the crew in the database, had isolated a few names.

I go to the com cab — used to be the radio cabin — but of course these days we communicate by satellite, even navigate by satellite. Still call the communications officer 'sparks', though. The merchant marine has its traditions, even if the rest of the 'world has gone tech crypto.

"Sparks," I say. "I need to talk to London but I can't get a clear channel."

Guy is English but was born in Bangkok. That's what his passport says. Probably Tai mother. We're like the UN around here.

He looks up from his monitor. He's wearing headphones. Can hear techno beats as he removes them.

"Quartermaster."

"What's the problem? Solar storm or something?"

"We're blacked out. No talking to anybody, Captain says."

I nod, say, "I understand... but this is Captain's business. Gotta talk to London. Buzz the X, man. He'll tell you."

Sparks does that and the Captain approves the link. I head back to my crib, log on, talk to Kelly at Control. Control is routed through the Union server, so looks legit.

"I got some names here I want checked out, Kelly," I say. "Lookin' for the usual cancer."

I feed him the names, all deckhands except for lst Officer Rublev. I think everyone else is kosher, just a gut feeling and... well, I have my reasons. I omit Iris.

Intel is always problematic. When we first heard about Moonlight, it seemed absurd until we got our hands on a strip, tested it and realized it was possible to bridge wire it into any electrics used by a car or an aircraft or even a cell phone, the obvious choice for ignition. Great assassination weapon, obviously. Who came up with it? Unresolved. The NK bandits were — and are — suspected, yet for all Pyongyang's ability for creating big bangs, their technical abilities ain't much. Everything they got is ripoff. They steal big, they steal little, like mice in the wall. Kelly said that, whoever Kelly is. I've never met the man. Better that way.

Did I check the Hirohito Lincoln for Moonlight? Wiring is too old. No cpu, no flash memory. Entirely unsuitable.

The Bentleys were clean. Conclusion: the Sea Dragon is just an old school contraband runner.

But what is Dazai up to?

I have questioned Iris. Again. Yes, in the back seat of the Lincoln.

"Baby," I say. "I'm wondering about the Captain. Is he making it up or did Dazai really demand that he turn the ship south?"

"All true," says Iris. "Dazai says we're meeting someone."

"In the middle of nowhere?"

"That's what he says."

"Tricky business off-loading 35 tonne tanks at sea. Makes no sense."

"Well, we're not going south... Captain has put his foot down. We'll be in the Bombal Channel as planned."

"Then what?"

"We get our money."

And everyone will be happy. Bullshit.

Anyway, when I finish messaging with Kelly, I get an unexpected visitor — Dazai. No white suit. Guess it was at the cleaners, if the cleaners on the Dragon could handle fabric like that. He's wearing jeans and a black T, could pass for just another deck scrubber who lives in a steel bulkhead with no windows. Still has the eyes of a Buddha, though... and the bland, ambiguous expression to match.

"A word, Quartermaster Caine," he says.

I'm twisted in my chair, looking at his hands, something I have noticed before but not comprehended — dude has 6 digits. Unusual, although not unheard of.

"I'm all ears, Mr. Dazai," I say.

"It must be obvious to you that Captain Ekzetera is unfit."

"How so?"

"He is deviating from the mission."

Of course I'm thinking — and you're thinking — do I really know what the mission is? I could ask him... but why reveal ignorance to a psychopath?

"The Captain is a little strange, I grant you," I say casually. "A bit Zen."

Dazai dismisses this with a faint smile: "Ekzetera knows nothing of Zen. He is *haikyo-sha*. He visits the wrong temple."

"Ah, an old problem," I murmur.

"You know he intends to sell our tanks to the Americans?"

Woa — this is a gobsmacker. But I play relaxed.

"I wondered about that... although I suppose their money is just as good as Chagos... maybe better."

"Money is not the point."

"No? Can I ask you a question, Dazai?"

He says nothing, just keeps his eyes on mine.

"What part of Korea are you from?"

"Nagasaki."

"Nagasaki... that's Japan, man. You're Jap?"

"I am Korean. My family was forcibly removed from Korea in 1927, sent to work as slaves in the Nagasaki shipyards."

"You survived the atomic bomb?"

"Well, I wasn't born then. Some of us died, of course. Thousands... many, many thousands of Koreans. A little known fact, Mr. Caine."

There's an uncomfortable edge to his voice, so I turn away, look at my computer screen. Mistake.

I say, "What would the Americans want with a bunch of old Korean tanks?"

No answer — at least, not then. Hear a cry, then a thud, as someone crashes against the filing cabinet behind me. Try to swivel in my chair but get whacked before that happens. A blow at the base of the neck, a very dangerous area. Lights out, baby. No chance, no escape. Suckered.

When I come to, I'm gagged with duct tape and hog tied,

hands behind my back, and hands tied to my feet, plus a noose around my neck that's tied to my feet... so if I try to straighten, the noose tightens into a choke on my throat. Bad business. Can still smell the world, can still hear the world, see it... but I'm not going anywhere unless it's in this lifeboat. The cutter, if I'm not mistaken. Same one I found Colgan in, back when he claimed he was attacked. Well maybe he was, and maybe I'm an idiot for not taking him seriously.

Sure, I'm pissed that Dazai got the drop on me, set me up for the sucker... yeah, yeah, "everyone's got a plan until he gets punched in the face blah blah". Except I didn't get punched in the face. My shoulder, neck, and spine feel like what a fish must feel when it gets chopped and sliced by a sushi chef.

But then, in the dim light of the shrouded cutter, I see someone else lying on the gunwhale. Pain or no pain, flash movies and scrambled eggs, I recognize Dazai. Tied and muzzled, same as me, but worse, 'cause he's not moving. I make noises, get none in return. He's looking stiff. Could be gone or close to it. Big surprise. I figured him for the hit... so, who got me? Us? What flippin' next?

You know how it is when you're all dressed up with nowhere to go — you think bad thoughts and bad thoughts become bad dreams as you slip in and out of consciousness. Maybe you dream about wife number one. I do. We walk to the bus stop and she gets on Number 38 for downtown, will bring her back before midnight when she's finished shopping, although she never does come back.

That part's true, the rest bullshit. It goes on in installments but you don't need to hear it. Made me cry, and who needs a sob story, even if it's just a dream? Moments like this, I could do it on canvas, hang it on the wall, be a famous painter.

So it goes, both of us laying there, no cheep from Dazai, and me incapable of escape. My muscles cramp and I'm crazy from trying not to flex and not tighten the noose. It happens, though. You can't help it. Just like that book I read on the plane to Tokyo: *Magnesium Deficiency & the Fall of the Toba Dynasty* — the imperial shoguns lose muscle strength through bad diet. Seizures due to premature aging brought the whole shiteroo down. Interesting theory. Big picture stuff. Little details matter.

Like this rope around my neck and throat... so tight now... can hear my heart thumping in my ears.

Next time I come to I hear the side thrusters kicking in and out, then the mooring lines running. We've arrived. A lot of metal clanking, then the tanks being driven off. They make a lot of noise. 35 tonnes, 600 horse power diesels. Probably rolling onto a deep sea scow. As the dawn starts to creep, so does the tropical mug... and the clamour of the jungle birds. Nice. Welcome to the Chagos Archipelago.

Then we get visitors. It's still pretty dark inside the cutter, so the first thing I see is a flashlight, then hear low voices as two guys make their clumsy way into the cabin. Captain Ekzetera and some dude who's dressed for action — boots, jungle greens and a SIG Sauer M17 service pistol cradled in a snug fast-action holster.

I pretend to be out of it. Not difficult. Feel the flashlight stroking my closed lids.

The voice is husky. Could be Texas.

"Who's this clown? We want him?"

"A professional saboteur."

"Yeah? Who he working for?"

"For me."

"So why the demotion?"

"Shelf-life, Major. Past its due date."

The flash light shifts to Dazai, who's still stiff and silent.

"This our guy? The Poet?"

"As promised."

"He's not looking so good, Captain. I'd say he was dead."

"Really? No pulse?"

He checks, grunts. Guess he doesn't know his pulse points.

"How we know for sure it's our guy?"

"Count his fingers."

There's a long pause, then the American says, "Six, including the thumb. Weird. Never seen that before."

"Nagasaki," says Ekzetera. "Inherited mutation."

"Isn't he Korean?"

"Oh yes, he's Korean. I believe he's considered a dual national."

"Dual? They're the fuckin' worst. The world was a lot simpler without those assholes."

"Indeed, Major. So, how much is he worth?"

"Nuthin'! Can get no info from a dead man."

"But surely there are things to be learned from the body."

"Like what."

"Proof of identity."

The American takes out his cell phone, takes a picture.

"Six digits good enough I.D. for me," he says.

Ekzetera is clearly disappointed.

"He has to be worth something to your organization," he says.

"Don't be greedy. Captain. You're getting over a hundred mil for the 30 smokin' commies."

There's silence, except for their breathing and the distant sound of the gentle waves of the Channel.

"Know what, Captain? We'll check 'em out, get back to you later."

"Fine. What about the saboteur? He's got secrets."

"Yeah? He can keep 'em. Let's go —"

They leave, then exchange a few words on the deck, close enough for me to understand.

"What do you need these tanks for, Major?"

"Classified. You care?"

"Professional interest, sir. I can get more... well, any sort of weapon needed for, let's say, a black flag op."

"Well I'd say you'd need a ship. The Sea Dragon is gonna disappear, right?"

"My backers have ships."

"We're not talkin' about the Poseidon Group any more, naturally."

"Naturally. Let me know about the Korean."

"I will."

"Soon. We'll be moving on."

"Well, I've got your number. You got plans? A vacation maybe?"

"Yes, yes… a driving tour. I brought my car, you know…."

So much for patriotic idealism. Captain Ekzetera is no son of Chagos. He highjacked the cargo for his own greedy purposes, screw the NK, screw anyone who though he was getting those tanks for whatever damn revolution he had going.

Their voices fade. Me too.

12: Six Fingers

I smell her before I see her.

"Koo koochie koo," she says, playfully slapping my face.

Alls I can do is blaze my eyes and make stupid grunts.

She's looking down at me like a cat with its prey.

"Idiot," she says. "*Manuke*. Didn't the Captain give you a gun?"

Yes, he did. But it was in the pocket of my jacket and my jacket was on the back of my chair.

She grabs the duct tape, rips it from my mouth. I'm gasping like a beached fish.

"Get this rope offa my throat!"

Her nimble fingers undo the noose. Sweet relief... but I'm still hog tied.

"Am I glad to see you, baby," I say.

"How glad?" she says.

Now, why do I say what I say next?

"Ekzetera wants to kill you."

I got no reason to say this... except maybe the guy is more jealous than we think. Or maybe I'm just trying to connect some dots. Iris always seems to be on the right side of hello.

"Don't be silly," she says.

"I'm not kidding, Iris. You're next."

She shrugs. "Silly. He's like any man — tickle his bottom and he's putty."

"You're the idiot, Iris — look what he did to Dazai."

Her large, lunar eyes swivel towards Dazai who's still laying there, stiff and silent.

"That's right, Iris — dead."

Iris shakes her head. "Dazai is very clever. He can be dead but not dead."

"He should be in a carnival," I say. "How about cutting me loose?"

"Why? I can do with you what I like...."

She laughs and straddles me, then runs her lips over mine,

and nuzzles my ear. Normally I'd be happy to oblige but now was not the time for Kama Sutra or family bonding.

"Fuck's sake, Iris! Get rid of these ropes, will you?"

Women. Like my 2nd wife when I broke my arm, said it made me look like a Greek statue. They always see a silver lining in our incapacities.

Ludicrous as it might seem, Iris just wanted to roll with me on the gunwhale like I was cuffed to a headboard in a bordello bedroom.

When she cuts me loose, first thing I do is check Dazai. Damned if I can detect a pulse.

"He's cold stone dead," I say.

"No way," says Iris. "Buddha say there are 9 states of trance. Dazai is a master of all."

"You mean, like suspended animation?"

"Yes. At least the 7th state, pure nothingness. Kick him, see what I mean."

I kick him and my boot just bounces back. No necrosis or molecular death here. Dazai is one weird customer.

"His father have six fingers, you know?"

"Yes. The Nagasaki gene."

"You believe that?"

"Why not? Cows born with two heads, right? Like Shakespeare say, life is strange."

It certainly is. While the guy was just as good to me dead as alive, I think maybe the noose should be removed, just perchance he wants to breath again, be alive. After two days you'd think he might need a piss, want something to eat.

I know I do. Fortunately the cutter is fully equipped, has a toilet and emergency rations.

Iris has brought me my jacket and my gun. Isn't that nice?

"I was in your cubby hole," she purrs. "I think, 'where is *manuke* hiding?' I go and ask the Captain and he says 'look in the big boat' where the Americans put him. So I bring your jacket and here you go."

Do you believe this? I don't. Possible, I suppose. But at this stage I still have no idea who bushwhacked me. Couldn't have been Dazai the suicide poet unless he staged his own incapacitation. Anything was possible, yet why get complicated?

Que bono?

"The Americans?"

"That's what Zee says. And you left your computer on."

The computer is the least of my worries. Or so I think.

"Your sugar daddy Etzetera tried to sell me to the CIA."

"He was bluffing, *manuke*. They want Dazai. Package deal. Let's go — he wants to see you."

Is she just being disingenuous or is she stupid?

"They don't want Six Fingers — they think he's dead."

"Bluffing. Art of the deal. Major Hammer has been convinced. We deliver Dazai tonight."

Well, the Major did take a photo. Maybe the spooks on Fantasy Island had a look, decided they wanted him after all.

Suits me. Tanks gone, cat's in the bag, bag's in the river.

I put on my jacket, put my hand in the right side pocket, feel the gun. Still have a pain in my neck and shoulders yet it melts away as the butt gets warm in my hand.

Over the on-board p.a. the 2 bells watch clock sounds. Five o'clock, which means it will be dark soon, and in the tropics I always feel better when it's dark.

13: Art of the Deal

"Where is my car?" Ekzetra shouts. "Who has moved it?"

He's looking up at the bridge. There's a big seabird sitting on the rail, doesn't budge when Rublev appears, looks down at the Captain.

"What's the matter, sir?"

"My car — where is my fucking car?"

"Americans took it."

Ekzetera's lizard eye opens up, looks hideous.

"The tanks, you fool. Just the tanks!"

"They said."

"Who said?"

"The woman said... the Sergeant, I think. She said the officer said...."

Ekzetera turns towards Iris, who's just a bit in front of me as we come up.

"Hear this, Iris?"

"Yes. They took my car."

First Officer Rublev might be pleased, although he has his usual sour expression.

"And they took the Bentley and the other car," he says.

"The Zil?"

"Part of the deal, *da... harosho spasibo.*"

I didn't care a damn about the Soviet Zil limo but I had an eye on that Bentley for myself. A 1952 R-Type Continental, very rare these days. Iris and I had a sweet time in that baby. Faster than the Lincoln, believe me.

Should've had the Quartermaster taking care of business, I think, instead of hog-tying him like a pig to be butchered in the damn cutter. Still, I do find a certain degree of pleasure in the Big X's outrage. Face twitching, spittle leaks from his twisted mouth. His pseudo smooth English leaves him and he curses in an unknown tongue.

He pulls his gun and I think he's going to shoot Rublev. Rubi certainly thinks so, backs away from the railing, just casually enough to save his dignity but fast enough to improve his odds on living. The Captain fires two, three shots. Sparks fly as the bullets ricochet off the steel plating of the wheel house. Nickel slugs, I'm thinking. One of them hits the bird, either by chance or by design, and the bird goes airborne, flaps its wings, stalls, drops to the deck with a thud. A frigate gull, can fly for hours in dirty weather if needs be.

Shame. Bad omen, as we all know.

Rublev is in slow motion. He's not reaching for the bridge door or trying to get out of Dodge. His face is tight, and all he wants is a cigarette. His hand moves slowly, removes a crushed pack from his shirt pocket, sucks a cig from it, lights up. His eyes never leave Ekzetera's.

Iris steps forward, grips Ekzetera's wrist, restrains him with a burst of urgent Japanese. His head turns towards her, the lizard eye ball fully exposed, then disappearing as his anger subsides.

I wonder how he came by it — an accident, a fight, or maybe he's had it from birth. It's like an instrument dial, a way of reading his mind.

Rublev flicks some ash from his smoke, leans on the railing again.

"Message for you, Captain. The Americans want Mr. Dazai after all."

This should make the man happy.

"They radio that?"

"Yeah. Major Hammer. They'll come tonight."

"Get my car back," hisses Iris.

"Can we catch the scow?" says Ekzetera.

"Easy," says Rublev. "It's on the radar."

"Still in the Channel?"

"*Da*. Moving at 8 knots."

Heavy load, slow boat to China, I think. In this case, Diego Garcia. What a screwed up operation.

"Catch up to them, Mr. Rublev."

"But Hammer says —"

"Never mind Hammer. Weigh anchor, Mr. Rublev. Catch them."

Marley shows up, just like he's been summoned by the Bridge. No smile, looks a bit shifty quite frankly. He's wearing a pair of blue rubber gloves. He picks up the bird by one of its wings, drags it to the railing, heaves it overboard. Notice he crosses himself quickly before turning away and going back to wherever he came from.

No singing, no Rasta Man shit now.

"I'm going to take a nap," says Iris.

And she too buggers off.

Now it was time for my conversation with Ekzetera. Who had suckered me and Dazai? Why the goddamn blunt force trauma to the back of my head? By the Captain's command, obviously. I knew that much from what I'd overheard of his conversation with the American Major. I didn't like it. I didn't like being knocked unconscious and tied up like an animal for slaughter, then offered as a meat side-order to the USA rendition boys. Sure, the Big X had given me five g's advance to play his game, but now it looked like I was expendable. Didn't matter what Iris said. Clumsy mistake by the muscle guy. Clumsy? Screw clumsy. That attack was professional.

"If he want you dead, you be dead," said Iris, sounding very Tokyo.

Maybe he was jealous, maybe he was greedy, maybe he was just plain mad. But he was professional and he had surrounded himself with professionals even if they fucked up occasionally. Accidentally on purpose like, eh.

"Captain," I hear myself saying. "I never had a chance to finish my research..."

We go to the stern, watch the wake that develops in a spreading white furrow as we get underway. Be so easy to shoot the bastard, drop him over the side, watch him disappear in the foam.

"Why was I assaulted and restrained like that?" I say thickly. "Not what we agreed, Captain."

"Had to do it, Mr. Caine," says Ekzetera. "Realism."

"I don't like realism."

He offers me one of those skinny cigars he smokes occasionally. I wave it off. He lights one for himself.

"More to the point," he says between puffs, "did you pick up any useful information?"

"Dazai isn't easily fooled."

"That's a no, then, is it? Pity."

"Yeah, pity."

"Head sore?"

"Sore enough, yeah, but not so sore I missed what you said to the Major."

"Realism, Quartermaster, realism. He's a crook. Has to be handled carefully."

"Obviously. He scooped your autos. If I'd been monitoring the off-load, that wouldn't have happened."

"We'll get them back."

"You know most of your crew are flagged."

"Meaning?"

"They're on everybody's list. Interpol, FBI, Israeli Intelligence... but you know this."

"I take what am I given, Mr. Caine."

"What about Mishima?"

"What about him? Was he flagged?"

"Didn't check. Just the current crew, as you requested."

I don't tell him I requested a special rundown on Iris. Doesn't matter now. I got thumped before I got to her profile, and of course the report was time sensitive, the file scrubbed automatically, leaving nothing about her or any of them on my computer.

Sic vita est — such is life.

14: The Archipelago

The Chagos is really a very pretty spot. Great biodiversity — lots of coconuts, lots of sharks. Be a great tourist destination except the islands are empty save for Diego Garcia. Lots of shipwrecks on the reefs, a few castaways over the years. Arabs, Dutch, Portuguese... then French, then British, now American, although the British issued the lease and Mauritius is claiming the whole archipelago with the UN and the international courts behind it. A mess, but a quiet mess until now. Rumors have Somali pirates working out of here and Chagoian guerrillas training in the jungles but this talk might be as fanciful as the talk about the return of the long extinct Dodo bird to the islands.

I once took a holiday with wife number two on the Seychelles, which isn't all that different from the Chagos, just a bit closer to Africa and Madagascar. Lots of empty islands, beautiful white beaches, creole population, and few *coup d'etats* to keep things honest, although I wasn't there to exercise my professional expertise in such matters. We swam, we drank, we argued, we fought. I got one of the worst sun burns of my life and I usually don't burn. We smoked some local weed, ended up separated and doing crazy stuff. Our marriage never recovered and that's all I care to remember. Maybe that's just the tropical way. Maybe that's why I'm feeling a tad uneasy when I should be wired, ready to rock 'n' roll. After all, I didn't get to sink the ship, so I need some juice. Should be interesting to see if Iris can get her car back and if the Americans really want the Poet.

We're closing in on the scow. Sky is heavy with cloud, the air humid. Could be a storm brewing but maybe not. In a hour or two everywhere might be blue and sparkling with brilliant sunshine. Or it could be blitzkrieg. We catch the SE Trades around here. Weather can change fast.

I sneak a visit with Dazai. He's awake now. No ropes. I don't bother to ask how or why. He's like Houdini, makes a living from cheating Death. Actually, they've got one of his ankles chained to a rail.

"Tell me, you got six toes as well?" I say.

"Yes. Problem with that?"

"No problem. But tell me, why did you kill all those guys in Singapore?"

"I follow orders. Don't you?"

"You don't follow orders, *amigo*. You're a poet."

The faint smile, the Buddha smile.

"You've been listening to Iris. Sweet girl, yes?"

"Sweet enough."

"Meet her mother?"

"No. You?"

"Oh yes."

"Do you consider yourself Japanese or Korean?"

"I consider myself a disciple of the Temple."

"And which Temple would that be?"

He's looking at me like I'm just a piece of glass.

"Are you C.I.A., Mr. Caine?"

"Nope. Just an honest-to-god merchant marine swabby."

"A contract operative, then."

"Sure, sometimes I moonlight."

"Interesting phrase, Mr. Caine. If I asked you to get rid of this chain, would you?"

"How could I?"

"You're the Quartermaster and the Quartermaster has keys."

This is true. There's even an emergency skeleton key in my crib, although we don't call it that. Master key is the preferred term.

"What's the beef between you and Captain Ekzetera? Iris?"

"Allow me to caution you about Ekzetera. He's treacherous."

"Yeah, I know. Wrong temple."

"He asked you to sink the ship, yes?"

"Why would he do that?"

"Because I know the correct destination."

"I think he was worried the crew might mutiny."

"All of them?"

"I was looking into that last time we talked."

"You can't find everything on a computer, you know."

"Who says? Buddha? Hey, I'm just trying to get some clarity before they ship you out."

"You too, *chingu*. Like Mishima."

Don't like the reference to my predecessor. Still, I smile.

"Who's the boss — Ekzetera or you?"

"He sold the tanks, yes?"

"Yeah, while you were sleeping. Americans."

"Not the correct destination. He's greedy. Has he shared the money with the crew? No? Of course not."

"Give him time. There's been a hitch."

"Oh, they burned him."

"Maybe. Can't say for sure."

"They burned him."

This is a possibility. A couple cars is one thing, full payment another. Far as I knew, he wanted cash in a suitcase, no magic digi in an off-shore account in some narco paradise. Since the collapse of crypto, nobody in the big league wanted anything but fresh Uncle Sams or weighted bars of Aztec Sunshine.

"Did you know Mishima?"

"Your predecessor? I knew him. Beautiful."

"Same temple?"

Dazai nods subtly, just slight movement of his very symmetrical head.

"Murder?"

"Perhaps a sacrifice to Susanoo."

Susanoo is the local storm god. Sea of Japan. Recognized by both Koreans and Japanese. Anyone who has sailed around there knows Susanoo.

I let him have his joke.

"They're turning you over to the Americans."

"So release me."

There were plenty of places he could hide. The Sea Dragon was a regular warren of cubby holes. But why should I? Would he be a friend I could trust? Of course not. But, on the loose, he might be a useful decoy.

"I give you something," he says.

"Like what, Dazai?"

"My cell phone."

"We're outta range, *amigo*."

He wags his leg, rattles his ankle chain.

"Mine is never out of range."

I go to his cabin. But all I find is a samurai sword. Can't miss it. Lying on his bunk, unsheathed. Could be a Mino but I'm no expert. Slim, slight bow, ready for whacking. Samurai *wakizashi* sort of thing. For a guy who uses grenades and is probably no stranger to 'moonlight' this seems pretty sentimental.

A Disciple of the Temple, eh.

But where the hell is that cell phone?

15: Burned

The evening air is thick with the sweet smell of the bird-catcher trees. Got another name but I can't remember it, just the fact that they can grow pretty big and the flowers go to seed and stick in the nesting birds' feathers, causing them to crash and burn so to speak. A few just die on the roost, hang from the branches like voodoo dolls. Some people eat the leaves, no problem. Wood is useless. Too soft to make anything but manure. They look good, though, and you get forests of them on some of these islands, just like the one where we finally catch up to the scow. You could swim to it, easy.

Well, they're waiting for us.

"The cars weren't part of the deal!" bawls Ekzetera.

He's standing in the mid-level loading bay with the rest of us. Open hatch. Maybe 50 meters from the scow, which is low profile compared to the Sea Dragon. Deck can't be more than 6 or 10 feet from the water. It's a reversible, meaning either end can be the bow or the stern, so tugs can just pull from whatever end is convenient. Lettering on the side says Trench Marine.

Major Hammer is looking back at us. He's on the lip of the end facing this way. Got his female Sergeant with him. She's hard looking — ugly hard, not like the movies. Bare arms addled with tattoos, shoulders like one of those tennis players who grunts every time she crushes the ball. Military haircut, military shades, and a military scowl. Diesel butch, maybe.

"I want them back," shouts Ekzetera. "Not part of the deal."

"Maybe some of my drivers were over-zealous," says Hammer. "Sorry."

"The Lincoln, the Bentley... uh, the Zil. They have to come back."

"Uh, no can do. They're at the rear... see?"

This is a problem. Not easy to move those tanks around, make a lane.

"The cars must be returned," says Ekzetera. "Especially the Lincoln."

"No can do, Captain. Sorry."

"I must have the Lincoln back. Understand, Major? Please cooperate."

Somebody — I don't know who — shouts, "That ancient pieca shit? Get real, Ahab!"

Hammer turns, looks behind him, snarls, "Stand down, jerk!"

Guess it's some grunt. Must be a few of them lurking among that phalanx of heavy metal.

The Sergeant shouts, "Send the Korean over!"

Naturally, Captain Ekzetera isn't agreeing to this. I'm wondering if he's been paid yet. Seems like bullshit to get bitchy over a couple of cars if you've got two or three hundred mil in your hip pocket.

The ramp is electric, although we have to bring the Dragon a tad closer to the scow. Fairly easy manoeuver. Rublev and Jurgens are on the bridge.

"You want the Korean, give us the car back, and you get him."

Dazai is part of our group but the only one with an ankle chain. He can move but it can't be fun. Colgan is minding him, and what a transformation for the big Belfast man, the reluctant 3rd Officer. He looks like he's ready for war — red bandana and khaki fatigues and a very ominous black assault rifle hanging from his left shoulder. And let's not forget the automatic pistol he has tucked behind his belt.

Well I have mine snug behind my ass but I have to say I'm wondering how many weapons the Captain has in that gun cabinet in his cabin.

When I look around, I notice a number of our crew are armed. Is this smart?

How many guys they got on the scow? Twelve? Guess they're all fully trained when it comes to using assault rifles and driving tanks. And if they're fully trained, they should be able to shift those T-59s, no sweat.

It's the female Sergeant who gets the ball rolling. Climbs onto the front tank with some skinny grunt who drops inside and fires up the engine. The Sergeant sits in the turret... and there's something about the way she sits that gives me a bad feeling. Could be Hammer, the way he's standing, the way he pulls a pair of glare goggles over his eyes. Maybe that dirty diesel engine noise gives me an Afghan flashback but whatever it is, I find myself edging sideways towards Dazai.

The tank centres itself to come up the ramp, then stops, and only a moron would think the raising of that 100 millimeter canon is just a rebalancing manoeuvre. There's a godawful flash, and a boom that rips my eardrums, makes me go blind as I get thrown across the empty car deck. Shards of burning metal shear this way and that, victims scream and the world spins. The second shell takes out the bridge, so I guess that's what took care of Rublev and Jurgens, as I never see them again. The ramp between the Dragon and the scow buckles and tears free as the ship pulls away like a wounded elephant. Through the open hatch I can see the scow, see Hammer and his Sergeant exchange looks and laughs, and as we drift away, Hammer gives us the finger.

This is what I will remember — not the treachery, not the screams of the dying, not the blood of the dead, but the finger. The tanned and muscled figure of Major Hammer giving us the imperial kiss-off. Not that I should actually care, as I'm not the one who got burned, but the arrogance of it pissed me off, more than the pain I was feeling, the noise in my head like I'm underwater and struggling to breath. The finger, man. Cuts like a knife.

But all this was happening fast, like a recap of a drama foretold. I black out. How long, who knows… minutes, not hours. No movies, no visits to the Underworld and back. Guess my electrics needed a time out.

Ekzetera is hanging from the pipes that track along the deck ceiling, looking just like a museum exhibit of some prehistoric bird, his arms extended like wings. His good eye is good no more and his lizard eye bulges like a piece of poisoned fruit ready to drop from its pod. The 'Big X' is really the Big X now. He's bald. Never suspected he wore a wig.

Where is Iris? For some reason I care. Too bad about the car but a body like that can always be replaced, no matter how vintage, how unique.

16: The Suicide Poet

Ping pong isn't my game, yet during this fatal voyage I've become something of an expert in the strategy of the back and forth, the nimble footwork, disguised moves, soft spins and killer shots, all this without lifting a paddle... until now. The game within the game.

So when Dazai suggests we play a game or two — something to pass the time, *chingu* — I go along with it. I'm not in great shape, but then neither is he. He still has the remains of the leg-iron on his ankle and he hasn't been eating, even though there's stuff that can be eaten, even though we've got no refrigeration, no power, nothing, and the ship is just drifting god knows where like a discarded tin can that should've sunk but keeps going, proof that all miracles aren't beautiful.

Getting rid of the bodies... that was easy, just over the side and away you go, fella. Some of the crew survived, of course, hail and fit enough to abandon ship as soon as they figured we were out of range. Colgan was a big disappointment. He took the cutter, him and Marley, and my measly five grand that made a nice fat role that fit perfectly inside a coffee mug I had parked beside the computer in the quartermaster's crib. Dumb, but who knew these pricks had eyes like orbiting satellites? And they made it clear they didn't want me along.

"You're bad luck, Caine," says Colgan. "Besides, I know you're the cunt who felled me."

This was preposterous but Marley backed him up on it, said he saw me do it. Subtleties of motivation are irrelevant when greed rules and lies come easily. Besides, I know about maps and charts, can navigate better than any of them.

"We all know 'bout you, boss," says Marley. "You're the guy who sank the Jane."

Those jerkoffs.

"I'm disappointed in you," says Colgan. "You came with great credentials. But you're playing a double game, Caine."

"You're schizophrenic," I say. "You drink too much."

Colgan gives one of those false laughs, half-way between a jeer and a growl.

"Listen to who's talkin'," he says. "Mr. Saboteur."

Marley taps the side of his head, says, "Music in the iron, quartermaster sir."

"The pot calling the kettle black," says Colgan.

"Not my fault you didn't get paid... Neeson."

Colgan has a fat smile, like the cat who gets the milk.

"I'll tell you about Neeson — he modelled himself on me. We went to school together back in Ulster."

"You can both act, I'll give you that."

"Not like you, Caine, not like you."

"Get a grip, Colgan. This is not the time for fantasy."

He's looking at me. A lot of measured contempt in those boozy eyes.

"You and the bitch."

"Yeah? Me and the bitch? Why am I still here, then?"

They exchange satisfied looks. Aw yeah, they have Plan B all figured out.

"Cause you be going down with the Dragon," says Marley. He sort of sings it.

Then I get thumped. Again.

Sour grapes, eh. They'd gone nuts looking for the Captain's payout, convinced it was hidden someplace in his cabin or what was left of the cabin, and when they couldn't find it there, they figured I must have it someplace. That's when they spotted the five. Chump change, sure, but just then the B-2 Nighthawk showed up again, made a low pass that scared the b'jesus out of them, and so they split before the Nighthawk could come back and finish us all off with a Hellfire missile or something worse. There were islands about, although the weather was shitty, the seas rough. Last I see of the swine is when their cutter disappears in the storm light, swallowed by a large trough in the standing waves.

Did they make it? I hope not. I thought they were my friends.

So all this leaves me alone with Dazai, the Suicide Poet, who's doing a fast, starving himself as a matter of Zen principle or something. When we're not playing ping pong, I climb through the ruined decks searching for Iris. I don't admit to myself this is what I'm actually doing because Iris is either dead or she escaped the ship when it got shelled. She's a good swimmer. I could see that when she took a dip in the Bombal Channel when we were waiting for the rendezvous.

I was still optimistic then. Thought I could bust clear of this scene without having to sink the ship or kill anyone and maybe Iris could be rehabilitated somehow and we'd go to Tokyo and meet her mom... who wouldn't really be a sly old bitch running a brothel that pretends to be a 3 star hotel. This is what happens when sex makes a sucker out of you. You're like a junkie, will do anything to get the fix. And my fix were the assignations in the automobiles of yesterday, the plush Siberian leather of the Zil, the polished Sherwood Forest fittings of the Bentley, and most of all, the ghostly, hallucinatory Detroit grandeur of the Hirohito Lincoln.

The Dragon is listing portside, subject to a sickening roll or two when a big wave hits and believe me, they hit. This is a Category 3 Tropical Storm. Been through worse, of course, but not in a crippled RoRo drifting without power and any sort of control. Tough to get any sleep, tough to figure out any plan. You just wait, pray for a crossing ship, an island, a helicopter... although no chopper is going to be flying in this wind and murk. Nobody's looking for us, except maybe for target practice, and that's just when they have nothing better to do. Besides, the satellites do the looking these days.

They have their tanks, they have their Black Flag ops... and they have those autos, even though they're of no use on Diego Garcia. Maybe Hammer will requisition a transport, load 'em up, fly them back to Texas.

Dazai, bizarrely, still wants to play ping pong, as if the lurching ship makes our game a ballet. I always let him win. I know what he's after: proof that he can still function as a super-being, regardless of health and the capricious vectors of the real world. He was never about the money or allegiance to Pyongyang or even a strange, malingering love for Iris (although no doubt he was her victim in their brief university days). Nagasaki. The ghosts of Nagasaki were in his bones, like the cries of the Zen temple gods that he evoked for his cryptic poetry. The guy was mad, yet had a way of making you uneasy, make you think yourself mad for thinking he was.

He told me the story of the tanks. Chinese, passed along to the NK, but here's the kicker: they were used as target dummies in one of the Red Army's nuke tests in the mid sixties. Lop Nur salt lake site — that's Mongolia, part of the Taklamaka-Kumtag desert belt.

They've got some archeological ruins there and mummies in caves, the sort of thing you see on the History TV channel when they're not going on about UFOs and hunter-killers in the bayou. Reds used a big white circle as a target for the air drop — Area D, they call it. So these tanks were placed around this white circle in a pattern like the arms of a spiral galaxy, so as to provide various distance impact data.

These T-59s were the survivors.

"Good intel, Poet." I say. "RGB?"

"My father."

"Your father?"

"Yes, he was a Sergeant in the Korean People's Army seconded to the Chinese. He was a witness."

Now I'm beginning to get it. This whole mission has been very personal for Dazai.

"Was he in one of the tanks?"

"A volunteer, yes."

"You're kidding, aren't you?"

"He survived. Left him blind. Nice pension."

Nice pension, bloody hell. Another bag of rice per annum, most likely. Still, he was able to send his son to university in Tokyo, so maybe the family did o.k.

So we play... and when we're not playing he's sitting on what's left of the main deck in the full Lotus position, regardless of the rain and the wind. He's shaved his head. Reminds me of one of those monks who set fire to themselves to make a political point. Why? Because he sits beside the large, ragged hole made by the tank shell, and that hole leads clear to the engine room, eighty or a hundred feet below, now flooded with a pool of churning sea water, purple and yellow and dirty gray with the slick of diesel fuel. Couple of bodies down there. Engineers, I guess. They should flush out to sea but they don't. Go figure.

The storm breaks after a couple of days and quickly everything is tropical normal again, blue sky, big sun, easy waves and white sands not so far away, as I can see the low outline of an island in the haze. Where are we? No idea, except we can't have gone far. Sun is still crossing high.

"Point Nemo," says Dazai. "We are close."

"Impossible," I say. "Nemo is just an imaginary place on the map."

"Maps are for fools."

He has pity in his voice. Guess his fasting has carried him to a different destination.

"So no map," I say. "How will we know?"

"Two moons," he says.

Two moons? He's mad. One of these guys who raids mythology to make a techno mysticism in the present.

"You should eat," I say. "We can leave the ship soon."

"You're leaving?"

"Sure. I can swim, can't you?"

Now I can see his eyes. Believe it's the first time I've really seen them come out of the clouds, so to speak. You'd think they'd be hard and homicidal, but they're not.

"There's an island over there, Poet... see?"

He follows my gaze.

"Sure about that, Mr. Caine?"

"We're drifting that way. Tonight we'll hear the surf."

"Perhaps we'll sink before we get there."

He has a point. The Sea Dragon has taken on a lot of water, is half submerged. Couple of car decks down and you're in it.

"Then we got no choice," I say. "We leave."

"Did you find what you were looking for?"

"The money? No, sir."

Now his eyes are concealed again and he looks like a monk, the kind who wear robes and carry incense. But that's just the face. In fact, he's stripped to waist, his pants loose and ragged, his feet bare, so he looks more like a prisoner of war, emaciated and passive, waiting to be shipped to Hell. The leg iron ring on his left ankle completes the impression.

"Another game," he says.

Is he crazy? We'll need our strength for the swim. Sure, there are lifebelts but you can't ride them forever.

He picks up a paddle, bounces a ball. Believe it's the only ball we have left. Well, what the hell — give the man what he wants. A whipping, right? So this time I don't let him win, crush him in two straight. Guess I'm exhilarated by the prospect of imminent escape.

He doesn't take it badly. When the match ends, we shake hands. His idea, not mine.

17: Diego Garcia

The moon is a classic crescent sitting beside a whiff of silver cloud and scattered stars where the sky goes black close to the horizon. A very romantic setting for the final demise of the Sea Dragon.

I got off. Dazai stayed behind, as I knew he would. Just him and that samurai sword. I had thought of shooting him, of course, because I did find my automatic in those final days of wandering the ship. Not sure if it was the exact one that Ekzetera had given me, as there were only two bullets left in the clip, and you know, as I never fired mine once, who knows? Two bullets. Maybe it was a message. Well, I wasn't into shooting anyone just yet. Besides, Dazai gave me his cell phone. I was touched. It was snug inside a tight plastic bag, and while it was of no use on the ship, there might be a connection if and when I reach the island.

I use the life belt to rest and watch the Dragon go under. Ten cable-lengths distant, far enough away not to get sucked under. Don't know if Dazai is alive or dead, if he used that sword in the romantic way, but he will be a goner unless he has something sneaky going.

the sea is a dungeon / full of groans and murder

Is that his? The lines run through my head as I watch. Don't know where they come from because god knows I'm no poet. Must be his, must Dazai's... not from his lips, maybe, but Iris'. Iris talked quite a bit about the Suicide Poet during our clandestine meetings, more than I cared to hear, truthfully. Well, the ship groans plenty as she disappears, leaving a slow spinning pool of debris. Interesting experience. I wasn't around when the Jane sank, just saw it on TV like the rest of the world. Chopper took us off, so I missed the final thrill.

And who sees this?

It's a long swim to the island and I'm knackered when I get there, embrace the warm friendly sand. White and sparkling as it slopes upwards to the tree line and the scatterings of palms and groves of Fly Catcher trees. So I just lay there for a while, get myself together. Watch a turtle come out of the surf, haul itself slowly up the beach. That's when I notice the suitcase.

A shabby suitcase, a thing from the twentieth century. No key, just spring locks. Sturdy enough though. Seem to remember a TV ad where a small gorilla finds it lying on the highway, tries to open it by stomping on it and throwing it against the wall of an abandoned gas station, all to no avail. It was full of money too, although what use is money to a gorilla? About as much as it is to a Canuck on a desert island, eh.

Sonofabitch. Was this the Big X's stash, the payoff for the T-59s? Had to be. I'd searched the goddamn Sea Dragon high and low, no luck, and here it was, another survivor just like me. Sure, the wads were a bit wet, but they'd dry out in the sun... wouldn't they?

Then I hear a car. Civilization. There's a road just beyond the beach and here it comes moving like destiny. I can hardly believe my eyes — the Lincoln! I stand there, the suitcase by my feet, my thumb out like the hitchhiker I used to be in my youth. The car pulls up and Etzetera gets out. He's still got his uniform on except his captain's cap looks like a chauffeur's cap.

It's not night and it's not day, is just layers of shadow, a world of muted color.

Iris is in the back, her face white like a painted doll. She's dressed in a red designer pant suit, the top a tunic, and yet the cut and look is traditional Japanese kimono. Masculine, maybe, and one might mistake her for a high-ranking business mandarin from Tokyo's Shinjuku district. But I don't. She's royalty, a princess with a princess's dog beside her on the seat, an elegant white collie with well-groomed long hair and red supernatural eyes. I just stare, gobsmacked, like I'm looking in a department store window.

Ekzetera takes the suitcase, puts it in the trunk, then gets behind the wheel, and they drive off. Me, I'm frozen, can't move, can't speak and they clearly don't recognize who I am.

18: Here Comes the Moon

There's something heavy on my neck and it's not a turtle looking for someplace to lay an egg. A boot. A voice I recognize says, "He's delirious."

It's Major Hammer, the prick.

A voice I don't recognize says, "Least he's alive. Recognize him?"

Hammer keeps prodding with his boot, says, "Yessir. Saw him on the Sea Dragon. The Quartermaster."

"Got a name?"

"Caine, I think. Yeah, saw him when we went onboard. Zetera said he was a sabotage expert."

"Moonlight?"

"Yeah. Pure bullshit. Guy's not in our database."

"Asymmetric?"

"Maybe."

"We'll bring him in for coffee neat."

I know what this is — coffee neat is a slang term for rendition. Assholes. Whose side do they think I'm on?

I can see the other guy well enough to recognize he's a big shot. A Brigadier General, a one star dude. He's got the tags.

"What about the others, Major Hammer — all dead?"

"Yessir... except for the 3rd Officer and the mate. They're cooperating."

Colgan and Marley. They made it... or maybe they didn't really. Maybe they're on their backs tied to a kneel-pray-bench with towels over their faces getting the water treatment. Cooperating? I guess they would be.

"What about the Captain?"

"They're saying Ekzetera is dead."

"Proof? Body?"

"Nah, he got smoked when we fired on them."

"Checked all the beaches? No sign of the Korean?"

"No. The 3rd Officer swears he's alive."

"Well if he was on the ship there's no guarantee of that

anymore, is there? Goddamn, Hammer, I don't understand why you didn't grab him when you had the chance."

"Sorry. My Sergeant was a little trigger happy."

"She gave the order to fire?"

"Yessir. This is what happens when we put women into front-line combat positions."

"No shit, Major. Hmm, this sounds like cause for a court martial or a promotion."

They both think this is funny. Me too actually, although with his boot still nudging my neck and my face stuck in the sand, I'm in no position to laugh along.

"Well, we got the autos," says Hammer. "Is there one you like, General?"

"Yes, the Bentley. Classy."

"I'd pencilled that one in for myself... but if you..."

"No no, you keep the Bentley and I'll take the Lincoln. Good old USA, can't beat it."

"Fraid it's gone, sir. Shipped out with the Japanese lady yesterday."

"What? She's gone?"

"Yeah. Caught a ride on a C-17 transport going to Tokyo via our base in Okinawa. Said the car was her mother's."

"Damn it, I wanted to talk to her. She's gone?"

"Yesterday. Part of the deal. She was a looker, I guess, if you like dragon ladies."

"I do. I was stationed in Okinawa for five years."

"There's always the Zil, General. Solid as a fucking dinosaur. If Kennedy had been riding in one of those, he'd still be alive today. Built to withstand an RPG. Belonged to Boris Yeltsin."

"Bad optics, Major. I can't ride in a commie limo, can I?"

"No, sir. I guess not."

"Let's go. Get the medics to collect Mr. Saboteur here, bring him back to the clinic."

"Will do. Too bad about the Sea Dragon but we got those 59s...."

I wait until they leave the beach, fade. There's a body in the surf, more turtles too. See some grunts way in the distance recovering bodies. Straighten 'em, bag 'em, tag 'em. Suppose I'm lucky. Maybe I can get my ass out of here before they get to me.

I roll over, pull Dazai's cell phone from my hip pocket, peel the plastic from it. I am lucky. It boots up right away. I punch in Kelly's number, listen to the rings. No answer. The rings stop. There's a strange vibration in the sand below my ass, and a distant rumble that actually becomes a series of rumbles, or should I say, explosions, a cascade of them that get louder and louder with every burst.

I'm very dim-witted, takes me a few seconds to recognize what's happening. A daisy chain, and this is no war game exercise.

This is 'Moonlight' and yours truly has set it off. Those T-59s must have been wired. No way, you think, too old? The cunning bastards had upgraded the electrics, easy as pie, and wired in some Moonlight... and it doesn't take a full moon to set that daisy chain off, just the code in Dazai's goddamn cell phone... and so who's the Suicide Poet now? Me?

You can imagine the damage at the base. I can. Thirty of those tanks lined up in front of a hangar or two or maybe inside them, a stack of B-2 Nighthawk bombers sitting nearby on their dispersal pad or in adjacent hangars... C-17 Globemasters... some F-35 fighters... Blackhawks, Chinooks... fuel bunkers... ordnance bunkers... any and all can be part of the daisy chain.

There's a huge cloud gysering upwards, just like an atomic mushroom. See it above the trees, feel the tremble. Distant, luminous, loud and swelling, another catastrophic explosion that will make the history books.

I know I have to get out of here before those grunt medics come to collect me. They have a cadaver dog, one of those shepherds that can smell a mummy in its tomb, so I better lose the beach. My mind starts running options. I crawl down the beach to the surf, dodging the turtles who seem to be congregating for a festival or something. Reach the body which is naked and missing its head, chopped off above the shoulders, leaving some neck but not much. I don't need to see the leg iron to know it's Dazai. He can't have done this to himself. Someone else must've have been on board with us, was still there when I abandoned ship. But who? The thought chills the mind, even if it's a cooking 100 degrees F in the world of the living.

This somewhat messes up my plan, although I go with it anyway. Pull back the six fingers of his right hand, then crunch them back so that they're gripping the cell phone. It's his anyway and it'll make a big mystery for the boys on the base and their spook detachment. When this leaks to the conspiracy crowd, yeah, it'll be a big big mystery with a million theories. Has to be some satisfaction in that, correct?

Meanwhile the air is an infernal roar, a mix of explosions, sirens, and engines... choppers, probably or *heelos* as the Seals call them.

It's not close, yet not that far. If I get up and walk a bit further, I might see the base, a perimeter fence or the famous dual runway.

It'd be a show worth watching, for sure, but I'm close enough, *amigos*. Close enough.

I get myself into the trees, far enough away from the collection detail. I walk a while, then lay myself down in the saw grass and wait for night. I came onto the island in moonlight and it'll probably be by moonlight that I'll leave it. Lots of time to think, lots of time to wonder who chopped off Dazai's head. Could the Big X still be alive? After his grotesque crucifixion in the steel rafters of the car deck, I never went back to that part of the ship again, figured someone else would take care of business. He was dead, no question. And my hallucination when I hit the beach last night and woke up in the dawn to see him driving the Lincoln, Iris riding like royalty in the back, was just that: a hallucination. There was no suitcase with 300 mil stuffed inside and I was no delivery boy. I was out of my mind, exhausted and raving after my horrendous swim through the reefs. Major Asshole said it: "He's delirious."

It was nothing to do with Iris, was it? She was gonzo. She'd probably driven the damn Lincoln off the Dragon herself, collected the loot, stashed it in the trunk. Was she still working in cahoots with Ekzetera? Did she twist the sucker, leave him to crash and burn still holding faith in her dubious loyalty? Or she likely swam ashore during the night. Never said goodbye to me.

So many possibles, so few probables.

Maybe Hammer left an assassin on board. But if so, why wait until the ship was almost sunk and Dazai clearly wanted to go with it anyway?

And there is another possibility — maybe he was beheaded on the beach. A Point Nemo moment.

And I wouldn't know. I was out of it.

Iris. The bitch had her hooks in me, despite her treachery. I was shaking with muscle fatigue and sunstroke, yet I was quite willing to suffer at her hands.

A new thing for me, this sickness. Hate, love and the desire to self-harm. And all I really want is to get off this island and go to Japan and hunt the beautiful doll down. One more time, baby. One more time.

Here comes the moon... and when the cloud thins, maybe I'll see the other, the one Dazai was so sure about.

19: Caine Gets a Ride

The Brits are so accommodating to strangers in need. Look at all those migrants they take in, a hundred a day average making it across the Channel, and no problem, here, have a fag, have a pint, mate. Saw one of their A.T.'s on the road, hitched a ride to their zone, and of course I was in their database. They talked to Kelly and Kelly told them, yes, he's in the Union... and so, despite the bloody mess that was confounding their American colleagues, they kept my presence secret and within a couple of days I was on an R.A.F shuttle to Singapore, then a regular flight to Haneda, Tokyo. From there, a short train ride on the Kyuko and I was in Yoko.

If you've ever been there you will have noticed the numerous residential graveyards below the elevated tracks, tucked between the skinny row houses. Small, jammed with tombstones, tight between the buildings like communal yards. Sure, you can see this coming into any major city someplace in this world, yet not quite like Yokohama, and if I'd been 30 minutes later, it would've been completely dark and I would've missed the show.

Makes you think about stuff, about risks, percentages.

But life goes on, and here I am getting out of a taxi at the Phoenix Gate at Motomachi Street, the upscale boutique and restaurant district. The steel bird sculpture on top of the symbolic gate is all lit up, looks like a constellation the way the out-stretched wings blend in a sort of ethereal way with the glazy night sky. But I'm not going up Motomachi. My street is further back, and a little less well lit. It's tight, the way Japanese urban streets can be, marked with sidewalk air conditioners and sagging electrical wires. Cars and motorcycles are jammed in along the way and the buildings bulge chaotically like they've been shaken recently by an earthquake. Here and there a tavern, an *izakaya* or a *sakaya* as they call them. Cats move in the shadows, the sky glows. Music cascades, drunks lurch towards the hidden moon.

Modern ethnic, somebody called it. The past leaves late and the future arrives early.

See the 'love hotel' at the end of a crossing alley. The Doll. Says so in red vertical neon, Japanese *Kanji* script, and in case you're illiterate, there's neon liner around the doorway. Looks like a keyhole but of course it's meant to be a doll, an *anime*. There's a big guy standing at the entrance, a 300 pound *yakuza* gorilla straight out of a Sumo wrestling club. Wearing a suit, so has to be the doorman. But more to the point, there's the Hirohito Lincoln, black and shiny in the light that oozes from this and that window nearby.

Well, I have a plan, and it doesn't include a conversation with the muscle at the door. I wait until he's distracted by a couple of hookers who wander up, stop for a chat, then I walk quietly to the car and get in. Not locked, not that this would matter as I have my Quartermaster's keys, can go anywhere. The car smells of Iris, just like she'd vacated moments ago. Soft, sweet, like cherry blossom as it falls from the tree. I feel below the seat, find the automatic lodged in the springs where I'd stashed it 'for future considerations'. A Hamada Type 1. There was a crate of them in one of those military trucks on Deck 13.

Check the clip — all cool. Then I loosen my jacket, stick the gun below my belt, settle in to wait. I don't have a chauffeur's cap, and I don't have six fingers, but I'm sure she won't mind. She can call me *manuke* or whatever she damn well likes. Just bring your suitcase, baby — I'm the 'Big X' now.

Turn on the radio. Works good. Forecast is for some rain, and a small craft warning for Tokyo Bay, winds 10 to 20 kt by midnight, continuing until dawn. Wind waves 1 to 2 meters, south flow. Significant swells on all local beaches. New moon at 12.

Hear a click as the door closes and smell that familiar Love Potion Number 9 scent the bitch uses. Iris. Caught me while I'm napping.

"Take me to the Temple," she says in Japanese.

I turn, smile. She's wearing that designer red kimono and looking like a million bucks. Has a bunch of flowers that she sets quickly on the seat beside her. Startled? Maybe.

"Hello, Iris," I say. "Time for a little prayer?"

She's good — she doesn't gasp or freak out in any way, try to jump out of the car, summon help or anything. Maybe her eyes flicker once but her face remains relaxed and confident, like she was expecting me. It's probably nearly midnight but hey, Tokyo Bay never shuts down.

"Mr. Caine," she whispers. "Back from the dead."

"Better believe it, baby. Where's the money?"

"What money?"

"My money."

"Your money? Don't be ridiculous."

"It's in a suitcase... millions... could be a half billion."

"Don't be silly, *manuke*. Hey, how did you survive the Dragon?"

Surprise, eh? Better question, how did you get off the boat... and hey, keep the Hirohito?"

She smiles: "I'm a woman. I have ways... I got lucky with the car."

Luck? I think. Luck had nothing to do with it. Bitch had the fix in all along.

I pull out my automatic, point it at her. "I should fuckin' kill you, Iris."

Yes, maybe she's afraid now. She's gone still as a statue.

"You sound mad, *manuke*. I'm really pleased to see you."

"Yeah?"

"Truly. I felt really lonely when I hear ship sink and you missing. It cut me, *manuke*. I cry. I took flowers to the shrine, cast them on the eternal waters."

"For me?"

"For you."

She's a professional liar, of course. And the way she slips into that baby ESL talk, geisha talk. Not working this time... or is it?

I wanted to believe her. The cars we rode, the pleasures we enjoyed, the undeclared bond that left us victims of the unknown. We were both criminals really... and crime... what is crime but a preemptive strike against Death.

"I'm willing to share," she murmurs.

"What's that?" I say harshly. "What?"

I smack her one — not hard enough to mark her beautiful lunar face, but hard enough to have me hauled in for some sensitivity training in that "other" world out there... although that's not the real world, is it?

"Please put the gun away. I said I share."

"Where is it?"

"Why you hate me?"

"I don't."

"You love me?"

Bitch. Our faces have been moving closer, eyes locked and closing. Rain begins to patter on the roof and the windshield blurs, the neon street lights going soft and abstract. I came thousands of klicks for this, swam the deepest ocean, and by god I'm going to take it.

20: The Temple

We drive out of town, to some neighbouring prefecture south of Kawasaki. Not that far but far enough on a squally night when the on-coming headlights mess with your eyes and you keep wandering over the line, wanting to drive on the right hand side of the road. Then the rain stops and the traffic is negligible. Hill forest, with occasional views of glittering Tokyo Bay as we gain elevation. There are holes in the cloud, stars to be seen.

"Why the flowers, Iris?"

"It's the custom."

I've seen it. Leave the flowers, wash the hands, ring the bell. At least she isn't pretending they were for me.

"I just don't believe you're religious, baby. I think you were going to meet someone, some pretty boy *yakuza*."

"Do you? I like that... I like jealous man."

For some reason her remark makes me think of the 'jealous god' theory. Worship no one but me, dude. I love you, have your best interests at heart. I speak to you in your darkest hour. Blah blah. Mnemonic flashback syndrome.

"Nice hotel your mom's got."

"It's ok. She's not well."

"Serious?"

"Some days she doesn't know who I am."

Yeah, like us all, I think.

"Dementia?"

"No, the other one. She shakes."

Hmm. Cry me a river stuff.

"Who's the big guy I saw at the door? Bodyguard, driver... what?"

"Shugoro. He's lazy, not helpful. He's supposed to make things easy for us."

"*Yakuza*?"

"Low level. Some *bosu* cousin."

"He drive you around?"

"Not tonight."

A car passes us at high speed, one of those sleek new electrics, so I never hear it coming. The high intensity lights were shuttered or something, maybe not on at all. Summer night, dawn not that far off.

Iris gasps, leans into me, grasps my arm. The Hirohito hits the gravel with a brief yelp. Bugger is sure heavy in the hands. No power steering.

"Asshole," I mutter.

"Could be cop," says Iris.

"Ghost car? Pretty fancy."

"He gone now. No worries."

Maybe so. To be on the safe side I chuck the remains of the baby bottle of Jack Daniels I was nursing.

Fortunately we got there without further hassles and there weren't a thousand steps to climb by flashlight. Had to be a park or a nature reserve, although it wasn't that far from civilization, was more like an oasis in the urban sprawl. Big trees and glimpses of a small lake, the sporadic cry of a night bird, a pleasant fragrance from the vegetation. Light was seeping in from the east. Must've been one of these beauty spots favored by the monks in the old days and maybe still was if I could see it properly.

But I can see enough to know there's nothing much left of the old monastery except one of those big *Roshomon* gateways near the shore of the black, silent lake. The moon appeared suddenly as if responding to some mysterious cue, and its perfect reflection was mirrored on the lake surface almost without blemish or distorting yellow pathway. Weird. The gate was obviously situated to frame this spectacle, and maybe the rising sun when it came.

Still, beauty and zen mysticism aside, I'm wondering why Iris stashed the loot at some raggedy uptown Shinto temple.

I could see why it was called 'Two Moons' and the spot would have some heavy sentimental cachet for the old school faithful... but Iris? *Manga* love doll Iris?

When the moon slides behind the cloud and the scene fades to black again, I say, "Nice... but is this it? Where's the *spondulix*, baby?"

She guides me to the statue of the god, which is standing in the enclave of a low cliff, partially concealed by hanging vines. XL size, 15 feet easy, minus its head, which is lying on its side nearby.

Iris drops her flowers at the feet of the ruined god, bows, then quickly washes her hands in the small pool that's fed by rock seepage.

Touching... really, I mean it. There's something pure about these believers, no matter how tainted they might be.

"You say this was Ekzetera's go-to place?"

"One of them. His favorite, maybe."

I remember. X said he prayed for success in business. Hmm... obviously didn't work last time, did it?

I'm looking at the detached head, running light over it from my cell. My muscles suddenly tighten, and I can't swallow.

"Dazai!" I croak.

Iris is inscrutable, says, "You think so... *manuke*?"

I was projecting, had to be. It was just the light and shadow, and the trauma projector in my memory clicking at 24 frames per second. I could see him on the beach, his severed head staring at me from the surf. But, but, it wasn't in the surf, was it?

"You shall not make yourself an idol, or any likeness of what is in heaven, or on the earth beneath, or in the water under the earth"

Goddamn, I was spooked. Snap out of it, Caine. Back straight, asshole tight.

"You kill him, *manuke*? You cut his head off, throw him into the sea? That's o.k. I understand."

Mind reader? Freudian gas-light psychology? Chick's a manipulator.

"We're wasting time," I snarl. "Where is it?"

"Please respect the temple," she says. "I show you."

"Good. Show me."

She shines her light in a gully, lets it play over the collected rubbish, and I must say for a Zen garden there was a lot of bloody rubbish... kids' toys, family portraits, coins, books, clocks, credit cards, clothing... samurai swords.. stuff, stuff, all precious once upon a time and now just a pile of rubbish glittering from the last shower to pass through.

Except... it wasn't rubbish, was it? Offerings, and because this was a sacred site, nobody would mess with the stuff. You'd be cursed if you did.

Her light picked out the suitcase way down there hiding in plain sight, just another personal item offered to the headless god. Crazy. Brazen and crazy.

"That it?" I say. "The blue hardshell?"

Fact is, there are several suitcases and because of the recent rain and muck, some of them look pretty much the same.

She nods, says, "I give it all up."

"Sure, sure," I say. "Fifty bucks, maybe. What did you do with the rest?"

"It's all there, *manuke*... I swear. I feel so guilty about all the shit and everything."

"Guilty? Gimme a break, you coulda cut off a finger and chucked it if you felt so bad. Tell me the truth, woman!"

"I tell truth... there it is!"

I really feel I'm being played, yet deep down I refuse to believe Iris would screw me over in the moment of our divine reconciliation.

"Ok, baby, I'm going down. Gimme light."

Bank's loose from the rain but I manage to slide down there without getting too messed up. Violation of a holy site? I've done it plenty in my time.

I crunch my way over the rotting and rusted, the recent and profane, the sentimental and precious, the whole pile of trophy culture alive with the souls of the dead or whatever love factor this stuff meant to the supplicants, get to the suitcase, try to spring the clasps but it's locked, naturally, is going require some brute force if my love doll doesn't have the key.

"No key," she says up there in the shadow. "Leave it."

Fuck that noise. I see a ratty short stroke samurai sword, grab it, put the tip of the blade under one of the clasps, start leveraging it when a bullet zings close to my head. I stumble, look around in the ghostly dawn light, fumble for my automatic.

"Drop the gun, Mr. Caine!" a male voice barks. "Drop it or die, sailor man!"

Do I recognize that damn voice? Dunno. Could be some ESL punk.

What are my options? A quick jump and roll to the left or right? Another shot, another bullet in the holy garbage at my feet kills that idea.

They got a light on me. I chuck my gun, the Hamada. Not out of place in the detritus.

"Wise move, sailor man. Now bring us that nice suitcase."

I'm looking upwards, can see he's big.

"Iris," I call. "You ok?"

"I'm ok," she says. "Do as he say."

Right. She's nervous, going ESL. Maybe she's part of the plan, maybe she isn't.

The suitcase is heavy enough, is loaded with something, and it's no easy task to drag it up that bank out of the gully. Well, what choice did I have? If you want to live, you eat shit.

I push it upwards and the big guy grabs it. Recognize him now — the guy she calls Shugoro, the muscle from the Doll Hotel. Not so big, fat and lazy now. Wearing a tight summer suit, latte color, and snazzy pattern clogs. Got a smirk on that baby fat face. Why not? He has the gun.

Iris looks sad. Her face, her open eyes and closed lips, say it's *sayonara, manuke.*

"Why Iris?" I say, looking up at her like a small, needy child.

"You not in it for the money," she says. "You in it for revenge."

In my conflicted heart, I know maybe she's right. What do I need millions for? The Sea Dragon was sunk, but I failed when it came to the cargo. Yes, I was pissed off, although maybe I was pissed off more because she had her hooks into me.

"You going to kill me?"

She looks away, says, "You like it here?"

"Sure... but it isn't home."

"Hmm, you no poet."

"I'm no Dazai, if that's what you mean. Hey, big fella, give us a hand, will you?"

I'm reaching upwards, extending my free hand, the other dug in the dirt to keep me from sliding back down. Shugoro is still smirking, still has his gun on me. I hear the dawn birds chattering in the trees. Could be a nice day coming.

What's really in that suitcase? A brick and a teddy bear?

Have both hands in the bank now because my feet keep breaking free. But when Shugoro lets go with another round, scares the b'jesus out of me, I opt for the old stuntman jump and roll... and this sends me tumbling back down into the sacred junk.

They're not trying to kill me — I was too close to miss. When I get myself together and on my feet, they're looking down, Shugoro with the dirty blue suitcase in one hand, his gun in the other. Iris waves. No smile, just waves.

Bye, baby.

Then they exit the scene. Casually, her hips swaying in that tight red kimono, and him loping beside her like a bloody gorilla.

Look around to see if I can find my gun, the Hamada, but no luck. See the suitcase I tried to open before I got dusted off by Iris and her goon and go to work on it, manage to bust the clasps. The big blood sun is rising over the far end of the lake, making it all prismatic and pretty. Look up, see the pale moon is still up there but fading into the blue.

Yep, nice day coming.

All that's in this suitcase is a framed photograph wrapped in a white silk dress. A couple with a kid, and the kid could be Iris.

Sure looks like her. The woman I don't know but she's a looker. The guy... well that's Ekzetera, isn't it? The Big fucking X! Smiling his big old *shogun* smile, except he's no *shogun*, he's *gaijin*. A foreign human from nowhere in particular.

So what is this? An offering to save the soul of the ailing mother, or the long gone Big X?

Toss the pic back into the case, close it, give it a kick, send it skittering across the refuse. What now, Caine? What now?

If I walk towards the lake I can get out of this gully easily, even if I have to swim some, but probably not, can get out reasonably clean. I stagger, slip, fall a couple of times but when I see the god idol, know I'm home free. Give him nod as I pass. If I had flowers, I'd let him have them.

I need a vacation. I need the smell of the sea. I need a regular gig on a sweet ship where the cargo is nothing fancy, is exactly what it says it is on the manifest. Some nice new electric cars, say. Environmentally friendly and if they should have the misfortune to sink mid-ocean some place a bit off the charts with those big old dirty batteries, who will give a shit?

I smile, nod to the idol again, keep going, eyes on infinity, mouth loose and ready for the first liquor I can find, even a jug of *sake*.